THE INVISIBLES

FLANNERY
O'CONNOR
AWARD
FOR
SHORT
FICTION

Nancy Zafris,
Series Editor

THE
INVISIBLES

stories by
HUGH SHEEHY

THE UNIVERSITY OF
GEORGIA PRESS
Athens & London

Published by the University of Georgia Press
Athens, Georgia 30602
www.ugapress.org
© 2012 by Hugh Sheehy
All rights reserved
Designed by Walton Harris
Set in 10.5 / 15 Adobe Caslon Pro
Printed and bound by Thomson-Shore

The paper in this book meets the guidelines
for permanence and durability of the Committee
on Production Guidelines for Book Longevity
of the Council on Library Resources.

Printed in the United States of America

12   13   14   15   16   C   5   4   3   2   1

Library of Congress Cataloging-in-Publication Data

Sheehy, Hugh, 1979–
The invisibles : stories / by Hugh Sheehy.
p.   cm.
ISBN 978-0-8203-4329-7 (cloth : alk. paper) —
ISBN 0-8203-4329-3 (cloth : alk. paper)
I. Title.
PS3619.H444I58 2012
813'.6—dc23   2011050391

British Library Cataloging-in-Publication Data available

CONTENTS

✧

Acknowledgments   vii

Meat and Mouth   1

The Invisibles   16

The Tea Party   43

Whiteout   57

Henrik the Viking   73

Smiling Down at Ellie Pardo   84

Translation   109

A Difficult Age   128

After the Flood   152

Ghost Stories   172

Variations on a Theme   190

ACKNOWLEDGMENTS

I gratefully acknowledge the publications in which the following stories appeared previously: "A Difficult Age," *Saint Ann's Review* 8, no. 1 (Summer/Fall 2008); "After the Flood," *Glimmer Train*; "The Invisibles," *Kenyon Review* and *The Best American Mystery Stories* 2008; "Meat and Mouth," *Kenyon Review*; "Smiling Down at Ellie Pardo," *Cream City Review*; "Translation," *Redivider*; "Variations on a Theme," *Crazyhorse*; "Whiteout," *Glimmer Train*.

I wish to thank people, family, and friends, for what surroundings and love they have supplied through the years; Nancy Zafris, for her eye and faith in these stories; the kind folks at the University of Georgia Press for their imagination and diligence in making this book a better thing; the magazine editors who saw fit to publish some of these stories; my best teachers, especially Steven, Keith, and Jim for such timely care; my parents and sisters and brother for the beauty and grace of your ongoing growth; Mike, Morgan, Neil, Nick, and Tom for the days behind us and the ones ahead; Anna, who will be able to read this before long; Katie, for all the ways you give the world back, for our dreams, and for things for which there are no words.

THE INVISIBLES

MEAT AND MOUTH

✧

Maddy left Luke Dixon sitting in the bully's chair and went to the Christmas-lighted window, willing the boy's loser dad to drive that blue Ford truck out of the woods. His lateness was eating into her weekend. Snow covered her solitary car in the lot, and she would have to dig and scrape before following the buried road from Grace Evangelical Church and School through the pale brown trees and bald fields to town. She thought of her apartment's stale heat, of marijuana buds in a medicine bottle in the freezer, of the cheap red wine on the counter. She was thinking of her records, of the jukebox at her favorite bar, of that bass player from Saturday night.

At a table by the board, beneath crookedly arranged alphabet magnets, Luke sopped dregs of Campbell's Tomato with a cheese sandwich. His excitement over a dollar's worth of food was as troubling as his choice to sit in the chair of Davey Schwartz, a larger boy who just this morning pinched and poked him during art until Luke clipped off his own paper Santa's head. Maddy had tried intervening, had tried doing good, telling Davey he would stay inside for recess. But Davey sniffed out her insecurity, like always. It was probably her imagination, but he had seemed to almost smile just before he went and told her coteacher, Hank Osmond. And Hank Osmond, predictably, had undermined her with the familiar head tilt that enlarged his jowl, saying, "Come on, Maddy, it's snowing," as if she habitually tormented the boy. Yet Hank had been all too happy to leave her alone with Luke, so he could get back to his surround-sound home theater, despite having recently told their director he had concerns about her temper. It had been a long week, and she was tired of male conspiracies. If Luke wanted to sit in Davey's seat, let him. You couldn't save them all.

Luke wiped his wet sleeve across his mouth and eyed his empty plate and bowl as if waiting for Maddy to notice and offer more, which would mean leaving the bright warmth of the classroom for the cold darkness of hall and kitchen, constantly bracing for the instant when the furnace clamored on downstairs.

"When do you think your dad will be here?" she said.

Andy Dixon was unemployed, and for some reason the kids all knew. Luke sighed, looking more sullen than usual.

Maddy put aside her exhaustion and stretched yet another smile. "It's okay, honey. I can stay here as long as I need to. Do you know if he had any errands to run?"

His lower lip began to tremble. She glanced at the window, pretended she had not noticed. "It's really coming down. You should eat some more before you go out there." She waited for him to finish sniffling and said, "Does that sound good, Luke?"

He nodded, then narrowed his eyes. His brow worked as if he were performing difficult calculations as he said, "Ms. Maddy, could we play a game?"

"Sure. What do you want to play?"

"I want to play pretend."

"Pretend what?"

He lowered his voice to a whisper. "Can we pretend I'm Davey?"

"Oh." She reached out, saw the greasy blue shirt had not been washed in several wears, then gave Luke's shoulder a light tap. Now was probably the time to give a speech, the one about the importance of being yourself or whatever. As if she never needed a break from Maddy, the twenty-four-hour mess who pilfered from her father's cabinets because the drunk tolerated it. "I don't know," she said. "Do you think Davey would like that?"

Luke's mouth dropped open. "It'll be a secret, Ms. Maddy. Don't tell!"

"Okay, Davey," she said, winking as she stacked his bowl on his paper plate, straining to grin. "If you don't tell, I won't tell. Come on down to the kitchen with me while I warm you up some more soup."

Luke shot to his feet and announced, "Davey wants chicken noodle."

"Well, then that's what Davey will get." She remembered something Hank Osmond said, that being a good teacher usually felt like it could get you fired. Watching Luke Dixon skip down the dark hallway to the kitchen, she hoped and doubted this qualified.

The building was shadowy and old, and the kitchen's steel surfaces and heavy-duty cooking instruments gave the room a torture chamber feel. While the microwave hummed and Luke cranked the steel lever of an industrial can opener, Maddy leaned in the window's light, pouring vodka into her coffee, planning to wash the mug at home. After a few sips she took out her phone and called Andy Dixon. When she reached his voicemail, she left a second polite message, letting the flatness of her voice speak for her anger.

"I bet he's in jail." Luke laughed like he'd broken a rule and gotten away with it.

"Why's that?" Maddy said, feeling thoughtful from her first few sips. "What would Andy Dixon do to get himself put in jail?"

"I don't know what he'd do!" Luke said, slamming the lever down. "Andy Dixon's a idiot!" With a burst of inspiration he added, "Andy Dixon's a fuckhead!"

"Luke!" she said.

The boy shook his head, his eyes bulging with excitement. "I'm Davey," he proclaimed with a shrug, and he began to cackle in a dry-sounding, high-pitched voice.

It was then, watching the child convulse and wondering if she had muttered *fuckhead* when thinking of his father, that she saw the man peering in the window at her. He was young with an unshaven, crazed look and pale blue eyes that made her joints stiffen. He opened his mouth as if to speak, then darted from the window frame. She hurried to the glass but saw no one, only the snow blanketing the playground and the slides and the woods beyond. Two sets of footprints crossed the field of white, one veering off toward the parking lot while the other proceeded to the window.

Luke was silent now. He looked at her, gaping as if he'd done something wrong.

The words to explain were out of reach. "Hold on," she said. Putting down the mug, she spilled coffee and vodka on the stainless counter. Cleaning it up appeared on her vague mental to-do list, just after calling 911, though before chewing some gum to cover the smell for the cops. At any rate, first thing was locking the school doors.

A second young man was standing in the corridor, his hat and face steaming. Maddy put out her hands and stopped, and Luke collided with her right butt cheek and hugged her leg. She hobbled upright and raised her arms defensively.

The strange man made no move to approach. Melted snow dripped from his long curly hair and wool coat. He was short and thin, with pale bluish skin and a pinched and hungry face. "Hey, we're lost," he said, enunciating with unusual slowness. "My friend and I, we're needing someplace out of the weather. Do you mind?"

The other one, the one from the window, was coming up the

corridor behind him, large and lanky in a black motorcycle jacket with clinking chains, one hand pocketed and the other a loose fist swinging back and forth. He was grinning in the same strange way, like he was on some drug. Meth, it's just some meth heads, Maddy thought with halting relief. They were meth heads on meth or something, probably harmless. She would make them all soup. She straightened her Luke-weighted leg and folded her arms, trying to not cry, to look like someone in charge of things.

"Did you tell her, Mouth?" The big guy elbowed the small one's arm. "Did you tell her we need out of the cold?"

"Sure did, Meat." He stared at Maddy in a semi-insulted way, as if they knew each other. "She understands our needs completely."

"Excuse me," Maddy said, the conviction dropping out of each word. "Do you know this is a school?"

"Fuck yeah," Mouth said. "I like totally did preschool here back in the day. Where's Mr. Osmond?"

"He went home," she said. "He's gone home for the weekend, and I'm afraid I have to leave soon, too."

"It's cool," Mouth said. "We can, like, lock up."

Meat pulled out his pocketed hand, and the cuff and hand holding a black object were smeared with red. The object was a knife handle with no blade. Maddy thought with cold clarity that this was a switchblade knife. The intruder was holding a switchblade knife. "This is dirty," the intruder named Meat was saying. "Where's a sink?"

"Whoa," said Mouth. "She's freaking out! Hey, don't freak out!"

Maddy backed into the kitchen, dragging Luke, and tried to unstop the door with the boy sitting on her foot. He was unbelievably heavy and resisted the hand prying him loose. He pressed his face behind her knee, crying through the denim. She let go of his short wiry arm and tugged at the lock-ring on the prop above her head. Meat with his bloody knife-hand was coming, his face growing flushed as he drew nearer. She slid the ring down the prop and the door began closing very slowly, and she pushed on the back of it to make it close faster. She shut it with his grimacing face behind the thinly latticed window and reached for the dead bolt as he kicked it from the other side. The bolt knob slammed back, jamming her fingers, and the door swung in on her forehead. Her head snapped back and she fell fast. She banged an elbow on the floor. The tiles were cold, hard, shell-green. Luke had let go of her leg. He lay on his side, stunned eyes blinking.

Meat stood over her, pointing the knife down, the blade unsprung. "Don't fucking freak out," he said. Noticing the sink, he stepped over her and made his way across the kitchen, calling back, "I fucking hate that."

"I know, man, but chill." Mouth came in, looking down at Maddy with a mixture of pity and reproof. "You shouldn't have run. We're not here to hurt you. You're really very low on our list of priorities. We have ourselves to think of."

"He has a knife," Maddy said by way of explanation. She reached out toward Luke, and he crawled over and lay on her shoulder, sobbing through her blouse, pinning her, though she no longer thought escape was an option.

"All we need is a place out of the weather," Mouth said, impatiently, as if she'd let him down. "You don't need to freak out. You're going to be fine. I'm pretty sure you'll be just fine."

Meat was running the tap, talking in a loud voice as he rinsed sleeve, hand, and knife handle. He sprung the long, straight blade and turned it under the stream, holding it until the dark stain ran along its edge red and vanished. "Clean, look. Like the day it was made, like the day it was born. Clean and new."

"That's great," said Mouth. "That's awesome news. I told you it would work out. See?" he said to Maddy. "Don't you see how it all works out?"

A techno song began to play, surprising them all. After a few seconds, Maddy recognized her phone's ring.

Meat stomped over and glared down. "What is it?"

"It's his dad calling," she said, her hand finding Luke's shivering ankle. "He's late picking him up."

"Don't answer," said Mouth.

"But he's coming here anyway."

"Then say everything's okay. But if you say something's wrong," he said in a slow teacherly tone Maddy had used many times herself and pointed his thumb at his angry friend. "Got it, teacher lady?"

"I got it," said Maddy.

"Go ahead. Answer it."

Maddy reached into her pocket as the phone stopped ringing. The two men looked at each other, and Luke let out a wail against her shoulder. "Shh, he'll call back," she said, then added, though she knew it was cruel, "Come on, Davey. Be tough."

The boy moaned and a second later the techno song resumed playing. She answered, feeling sober, fully in control of her voice. She glanced up at the intruders, saying, "Mr. Dixon, there you are."

"Hey, Miss Maddy," Andy Dixon said in an I'm-busy-driving voice. "Hey, sorry I'm so late coming to get him. I had a chance to get some work out on this house this morning and couldn't pass it up. Afterward, the foreman started cracking beers, and I didn't want to be rude."

She ignored his preposterous logic, saying, "It's fine. Everything's fine. We're waiting."

If he heard any fear breaking through her voice, he gave no sign of it. "Okay. See you in fifteen."

"Okay, bye," she said, though the call had ended.

"What's going on? What did he say?" Mouth said. "Is he coming?"

"Fifteen minutes," said Maddy. Feeling her forehead wet, she reached up and took away blood on her fingertip. "He drives a blue truck. No surprises. I'll tell you everything in advance."

Mouth turned and looked at Meat, staring until the bigger man lowered his eyes.

"You got yourself to blame for that cut," Mouth told Maddy. "Better hurry up and get clean before Daddy gets here. And get him calm." He held out his hand and shook his head when Maddy reached to take it. "Give me the phone, dummy."

They went back to the classroom, and Maddy went into the bathroom and bent at the miniature sink to examine her forehead in the mirror. The break in the skin was tiny, with a faint round bruise behind it. As she rinsed it and pressed a damp, brown-paper towel to it to stanch the bleeding, it occurred to her that the bathroom key was in her pocket. The door was reinforced with steel, and she doubted the intruders would be able to break it in if she locked it. She tried to imagine the various outcomes. The meth heads or killers or whatever they were tortured Luke until she came out or they killed him or they let him live and fled. They gave him to his father and tried to break in or took off. They killed Andy Dixon and Luke but not her. They killed her and nobody else. She fixed her hair and went out. They were all standing by the toy chest in the corner. Luke was holding a large plastic dragon. He was staring at her, terrified.

"Come on," said Mouth. "Isn't that like your favorite toy? It's the best one for sure."

"Go on," Meat urged the boy. "Do your thing."

Both men were frowning.

"He's scared of us," Mouth observed. "We've really got him

rattled over here. This one's got weak boundaries, for sure. Not a good sign, not a good sign at all."

"This kid sucks," said Meat. "Fucking waste."

"You'd probably be scared, too, man. Imagine if two big dudes came in and scared your schoolteacher. He doesn't know he's going to be just like us some day. You don't know that yet, kid, do you?"

"If we were kids, I'd hate him," Meat said. "Kick his ass and shit."

"We should come up with a story, guys," Maddy interrupted, smiling to show that, whatever they were on, she was willing to help, so long as they didn't hurt her. It reminded her of high school, driving friends on acid around the woods. She studied Luke. "I know we can trust Davey to keep a secret. Isn't that right, Davey?"

His eyes fixed with vague understanding, he nodded slowly and carefully.

"Why'd you say his name?" Meat wanted to know.

"It's a teaching tactic or something," said Mouth. "There's like a whole psychology."

"Is there like a psychology, Mouth?"

"Fuck you, Meat, you fucking lunk. You slab."

"Kick your ass, dude."

"You two should be our visiting teachers," Maddy said. "What are your names?"

"Tell him my name is Mr. Mund," said Mouth. He smiled around proudly. "That's German, you know."

"Fuck this," said Meat. "Fuck that." He turned and stalked solemnly toward the door.

"Where are you going?" said Mouth.

Meat stopped at the door and pointed back angrily. "Fuck you. I'll watch." The sound of his breathing faded as he went down the hall, and soon he appeared outside the window, crossing the parking lot through falling snow until he stepped into the woods, moving among the trees until he was out of sight.

"Somebody's in a bad mood," said Mouth. "Fucking asshole." He eyed Luke. "Sorry. Frigging jerkwad."

"It's fine," Maddy said with false enthusiasm. "Let's finish our story. You're a student teacher, just here to observe today. You're from the university."

"Sweet," said Mouth. "I'm Mr. Mund, the student teacher. I wish there was another chick student teaching. All the student teachers we had when I was a kid were foxy."

"He's the student teacher." Maddy sent Luke a telepathic message to keep playing, to be brave, just a bit longer. She wondered if he received it. "You got that, Davey?"

Luke nodded and tried to smile, though he was pale and looked like he might throw up.

The minutes passed slowly, ticking loudly on the old analog clock above the door. Mouth leaned against the wall, looking bored with both Maddy and Luke. Ten minutes passed, thirteen, fifteen, seventeen. Maddy began to think Andy Dixon would never arrive, that she and Luke had somehow been left in a parallel universe, and Andy Dixon would arrive at another Grace Evangelical Church and School and find it locked and dark. He would call Hank Osmond, who would have already forgotten Maddy and Luke, and the police would find no record that either of them existed. In his bewilderment Andy would visit Maddy's father, a haggard drinker who, after listening to Andy Dixon's story, would bloodlessly explain that his wife was dead, that he had no daughter, and that he'd never heard of Luke Dixon. Gradually it would dawn on Andy Dixon that he was free of his son, that he could grieve as little as he could stand. Meanwhile, she and Luke would be trapped here, with Mouth and Meat, in an eternal snowstorm. At least I'm not alone with them, she thought with a glance at the boy, though she knew it was selfish.

Headlights shined through the deepening blue air and falling snow. The pickup truck swerved quickly across the lot, stopping just outside the front doors, where usually the children stood in a group waiting for their rides. Without turning off the engine, Andy Dixon climbed out of the driver's side door, slipping in the snow, nearly going down on the snowy pavement. He stood upright and looked in at them, waving his hand high in the air, his face boozy and pink.

He came in smelling of timber and whiskey and bar smoke and reached out to his son, who ran up into his arms as if to the ladder of a piece of playground equipment. That was unusual, but Andy Dixon seemed too zotzed to notice. "Luke my boy," he said, then looked at Maddy with glossy red eyes, blinking, not noticing the cut on her head. Behind him, Mouth grimaced as if reappraising her character.

"Thanks for watching him. I won't let it happen again."

She put clenched fists on her hips, saying, "It's fine. But I do want to get out of here before the roads get much worse, so if you don't mind . . ." She gave a tight smile, then saw him looking with mild confusion at Mouth. "This is Mr. Mund, our student teacher."

Luke buried his face in his father's Carhartt jacket. Andy shifted his head and freed up a hand to introduce himself. "Andy Dixon," he said. "Pleased to meet you."

Mouth narrowed his eyes. "Nice to meet you. Hank Osmond says good things about you. Says you're a stand-up father. Glad you finally made it."

"Sure, sorry about that." Andy frowned. "You're a teacher here?"

"I specialize in teaching the kids strong boundaries," Mouth said. "Can't get ahead in this world with weak boundaries. With those, pal, you're nowhere." Mouth made a swift, cutting motion with his hand.

Andy was looking at him more closely now. "I don't get it. What boundaries?"

"Mr. Dixon," said Maddy. "Please. It's late."

"Okay." He gave Mouth a final, doubting look and turned away. He smirked down at Luke, who pressed his face harder into the rough jacket. "Have a good weekend."

She watched them go, aware of Mouth's trembling hands and the way he was staring intently. "Don't worry," she said when they had gone down the hall. "Andy's too drunk to believe whatever Luke tells him. And even if he did, he won't remember it."

"I thought you said the kid's name was Davey. I thought you were going to tell us everything," said Mouth harshly. No longer leaning against the wall, he took a few steps toward her, raising his shoulders, his warm breath smelling of rot from several feet away. "Why should I believe you at all?"

He smelled like melted snow, like minerals and dirt, like the things that lay in the earth, shifting slightly from season to season, sorted by gravity and flow. She stiffened. She felt quite dizzy. Behind Mouth, outside the window, Luke climbed into the truck, and Andy Dixon stood by his door picking snuff out of a plastic tin. Meat had emerged from the woods and was walking up behind him rapidly, his knife in hand, blade sprung. There was no sound as he wrapped a forearm over Andy's face and tilted his head back, exposing his whiskery neck. Meat drew the blade across the exposed throat, leaving a red line which widened and wept dark red down the front of Andy's jacket. Andy's hands fell to his sides, dumping shredded black tobacco into the snow. Andy dropped to his knees and fell facedown in the snowy lot. He never struggled. It was as if he had felt nothing, as if the life just spilled out of him in a growing dark spot in the snow.

"Don't," Maddy said quietly to Mouth. Outside Meat opened the passenger door and took Luke Dixon by the hand to lead him back inside. "We don't even know who you are. We can't tell the cops anything."

Mouth twisted his lips into an expression of disgust. "Shut the fuck up. You're a fucking liar. That truck is going to get us a lot farther than your shitty little car."

"Oh my God," said Maddy.

"Cut it out," said Mouth. "Lying bitches make me sick. I can't even believe a word you say."

Meat came in with Luke and let the child stagger to her. She heaved him into her arms and felt he had wet himself. He was shivering and pale, his pupils dilated to different sizes, his arms hanging limp.

"Kill them or what?" Meat said.

"I hate killing a kid and a chick. Makes me all queasy." Mouth scowled at them. "Put them downstairs. I hate phony bitches."

High in the wall a small window looked out at ground level over gathering ridges of snow, up at snow falling through gray sky and trees. It was colder down here, but at least the men had gone. She imagined them on the interstate, Mouth driving, complaining about Meat's choice of radio station.

She sat against the silent furnace, cradling Luke in her arms. Darkness hid his face, and she wondered whether he slept, or if he stared into shadows, too. She adjusted her arm, and he pressed a cheek to her ribs, conforming to shape and body warmth. They had only to last the night. The minister would arrive in the morning. Even if the Saturday service was cancelled for weather, and she suspected it would be, someone would come by to check on the building. And maybe they would be lucky, and a policeman would drive by before then, planning to hide on the job for a while, and see the lights on in the building and come close enough to see the body in the snow. Or, if the killers had moved it, there would be a lot of blood. Unless new snow had buried it. She imagined Hank Osmond driving back in the morning to check on the school, to ensure she had locked up properly. She could not put it past him, though she did not wish this discovery on him. However it went, things would go differently between them now.

A loud bang sounded within the furnace, and the pilot light flared up. Luke started, and she moved her hand to his head, lightly rubbing his scalp, letting him know she was there, watching over. The air warmed and he began to relax. She thought of her quiet apartment. In her bar, they were shouting over the music and each other's voices. A few miles away, in the house where she'd grown up, her father was drinking, listening to forty-year-old songs. How unbothered he would be, were he to call or find her not home and go days without hearing back. He would make this a gift to himself, a new reason to blame himself, a fresh cause to seek oblivion.

The boy whimpered softly, and when she touched his head and he sighed, she knew he was asleep and dreaming. She was glad he was able. He had a mother somewhere, but more likely the grandparents he sometimes talked about would take him. She supposed he would never return to this school, that after tonight she might not see him again, except to glimpse him around town and track his story as he claimed whatever space he could, a loner or a drinker, a criminal, a nobody, a bungler like his dad. Or maybe he would beat the odds, materialize triumphant from the cloud bank of the past, stun her and everyone else. Or maybe just everyone else. Whatever he became, she would not hold it against him. It was a long way off.

The basement was getting warm. For the first time since being locked down here, she felt the exhaustion in her neck and shoulders. She knew she must be hungry, but her stomach had clenched shut. She was almost comfortable. She would sleep through some of this, maybe all the way through, and in the morning she would find a way out. The furnace fired steadily. It was strange to think, down there in the dark, how lucky she was.

THE INVISIBLES

The end of my fifth summer singled it out forever in the stream of my childhood. Many days my mother and I cooked canned soup on a toy stovetop in our basement, pretending bombs had ruined the upstairs world. And one afternoon at the zoo, surrounded by wild animals in cages and tamer ones in trees, my mother confiscated my snow cone and yanked me behind a hedge. She crouched down and directed my attention to a small, gray-haired woman standing in front of the lions. Her face was wrinkling, rendered sexless by neglect. Families passed without the faintest interest in her.

"Cynthia, see her. She's more or less invisible, except to the lion, who sees lunch. She's not really invisible, but she might as well be. Wipe away that smile, little girl. We're exactly like her."

My fascinated mother drank from the snow cone until her lips were stained purple. She scowled and jerked her head toward the woman—the invisible, a person who is unnoticeable, hence unmemorable. Mother knew all about invisibles and kept her eyes open in public. She brought home reports: a woman licking stamps at the post office, an anguished old man in line at the bank, a girl crying by a painting in the museum. The library crawling with them.

"Remember, Cynthia, you're an invisible, too," she said. "Just like me. We're in it together. Forever."

That summer I collected her sayings and built a personality with them. I mastered my bicycle and braved the creeks and abandoned barns that lay within an hour's journey of home, never doubting that if a bad guy appeared, he wouldn't see me and, if he happened to be an invisible, that I moved in the aura of my all-knowing mother. Then, one August day when the corn crop was blowing, giving glimpses of sweet ears ripe for the picking, she disappeared from our house.

Over a decade after she vanished, a strange van appeared in the old parking lot at the Great Skate Arena. At once I knew an invisible drove the thing. Around the corner, in the main lot, honking cars inched forward. The grouchy cop waved his ticket book at drivers seeking a place to release excited children. No one had noticed this van, faded maroon with a custom heart-shaped bubble window on the passenger side near the back. Scabs of rust clung to the lower body, over new tires. It wasn't the sort of car you liked to see outside a skating rink or anyplace where the typical patron was twelve years old.

"First of all it should go without saying that a guy drives that thing. But mainly I wonder how he it got into the lot." Randall was our tall, brainy boy. He lived for logical problems like this one; the old parking lot where we smoked was separated from the new parking lot by a row of massive iron blocks with thick cable handles that only a crane could have lifted. The back of the old parking lot was closed in by a tangle of vines and meager trees. Beyond this dark thicket, from below, came the sounds of the highway.

"He must have come from down there." Brianna squinted at the wall of vegetation. I'd put the purplish paint around her eyes. "There must be a bare patch we can't see."

"I would bet that a pervert drives that baby," Randall observed of the van.

"Vans are too obvious for pervs these days." Brianna took a stance in her vintage black and white stockings. She was little, hot, and adept at finding killer vintage clothes in thrift stores. "He's probably some poor escapee from the psycho ward."

They turned to me to decide, these two kids who didn't know what invisibles were, even though they were in the club. They bore the symptoms of invisibles in denial, dying their hair black, punching steel through their lips and nostrils, wearing shirts that pictured corpses. They hung out with me. We hung out at a skating rink with junior high schoolers. No one ever caught us smoking. The list went on. Rather than try to explain our metaphysical plight—I'd never been comfortable talking about my mother—I shrugged, faked a smile, and ignored the sickening presence I sensed in the van's heart-shaped window. The mind I detected in that window was that of an all-knowing bully waiting for you to contradict him. "I don't know, but he's probably sleeping in there, and either way we don't want to wake him up. Can we go inside now and skate?"

I puffed at my cigarette between breaths, trying to hurry things along, confident that under the dome of the skating rink I'd shake my fear that a knife-swinging but otherwise unremarkable oddball lurked behind one of the dormant air-conditioning units lined up behind the skating rink.

Randall absentmindedly played with his recent nose piercing. "Look at that creepy window. If he's in there he's probably watching us right now."

Through the dusty window we could see the surface of an opaque space. In our own ways we acknowledged the disadvantage of the unknowing souls we'd spied on from behind unlighted glass. Our spines all twitched a little.

"You think he's in there?" Brianna pinched a cigarette above the filter, breaking it as she sometimes did when she was nervous. She let it fall on the cracked lot. Her voice grew quiet. "Why would someone want to sleep here?"

Randall walked over to the van and knocked three times on the heart-shaped window. Against the thick, curved glass, his knuckles made a hollow sound that echoed in my chest. Doing a good job of looking unafraid, he stood looking up at it, then smiled at us. Brianna and I watched the window for a terrible face.

Randall threw back his head and laughed like a cartoon villain who has just tied a woman to train tracks. Even at his most raucous he couldn't draw attention from the main parking lot. He cackled until Brianna snapped another cigarette in her shaking hand, and I put my arm around her tiny shoulders. She looked so helpless, her lip shaking, her stick palm dotted with tobacco.

"You're such an asshole," she blurted. "I'm not going to couples-skate with you if you don't come back right now."

"Okay, okay." Randall returned to the little field of safety we seemed to occupy between the brown steel door and the dormant air-conditioning unit. Above our heads, a light snapped on, and I could see how pale my friends looked, how afraid, and knew they could see it in my face, too. Randall squeezed between our bodies, with an arm for each of us. "Shall we?"

As if he could make us forget the unknown behind the dark window in the maroon travel van, he ushered Brianna and me toward the entrance around the corner, where, if she recognized us each Thursday night, the obese woman in the ticket booth would give no sign.

My mother had bad habits which arose as a result of being an invisible. She stared at strangers. She burst into laughter. These were marks of her frustration. She liked to tell cashiers that she'd already paid and make them admit that they hadn't been totally attentive. Then she'd give the money back.

One day my father and I came home from the farmers market to a house that bore all the signs of her presence. The garage door was open, revealing the backside of her blue sedan. In the oven, cooked blueberries pushed through the flaky crust of an unwatched pie. Suspecting she was hiding in one of her usual places, I parted the dresses in her closet and looked under my parents' tightly made bed. Outside my father walked the rows of the well-tended vegetable garden, and I balanced myself on the patio rail and stood, searching for her face in the field of swaying cornstalks that enclosed our house. Hiding was a game we played together, and with each shift of my eyes I expected to find her grinning among the rows.

When we grew tired of shouting for her, we went into the house, set the pie out to cool, and waited for her to emerge. I was excited to learn what new hiding spot my mother had found, but my father was upset over her absence. He slumped beside me on the couch and pinched the bridge of his nose. A fidgety, bald-headed man who knew numbers and tax laws, he was always forcing himself to keep his mouth shut around his wife.

The detective we spoke to offered no answer.

"Sometimes people disappear out of their lives," he said. He kept a neat steel desk with a rectangular wire basket on one corner beside his computer monitor. Beneath a glass reading lamp he'd arranged a scene with cast-iron miniatures, an eyeless, large-chinned policeman interrogating a tied criminal who glared up with red eyes. "They just vanish, you know what I mean."

"Not like this," said my father. The very suggestion she'd left infuriated him. "That's on the highway, on long road trips. Hitchhikers disappear." He didn't quite look at the policeman, directed his ire internally. His entire forehead seemed to throb. He held my hand with incredible gentleness.

The detective tried to disguise his pity with a perplexed smile. He looked at me as if reading my thoughts, then reached for a

Rolodex. "I can direct you to someone who's good at talking about this sort of thing."

My father flinched away from these words, said no, thank you.

Early that winter my father told me not to expect her to come home. I stopped asking him about it but continued to watch milk cartons and mail flyers for her face. I'd just begun kindergarten and wanted to tell her she had been right all along. I was an invisible. My new teacher couldn't bring herself to remember my name. Other children never looked at me and seemed to avoid the spaces where I played at recess. I was stuck wearing my name written on a construction paper label strung around my neck with yarn, long after the teacher had memorized my classmates. For weeks I felt like a unit of space in which a sign floated: "Cynthia invisible here."

My mother would have laughed. But by then it was just me and my noninvisible father and the noninvisible woman who had begun to hang around, in a restored farmhouse out in the cornfields that ran to forgettable stretches outside the city.

After the rink let us out with a drove of children to waiting parents, Brianna and Randall left in his car to go screw in their latest secluded spot. With a mild case of virgin's blues, I drove off alone, with a scentless, yellow, leaf-shaped air freshener swinging above my head. My drive toured the well-lighted streets of suburbs, and no headlights followed long enough to make me more than a little cold. For a few years now my fear of the dark had been completely relocated to a fear of people and especially to the signs of them in the dark, like the headlights of solitary cars and the sound of footsteps on a sidewalk. The full, rustling fields of corn I drove among on the road to my township had long been reassuring company. Though I'd seen enough horror films to envision the travel van pulling out of the vegetables, I'd ceased to think much about it.

Before leaving the rink I'd checked the old parking lot and seen only weeds bent to the gravel by new autumn winds. I'd asked the police officer who oversaw Great Skate's traffic if the van had been towed. A tall, sour-mouthed man with a crab-red face, he considered me as if I'd claimed to have seen a UFO.

"What van?" he said. "I've been here all night, and there hasn't been any van. Believe me, I would have noticed a van like that."

"Never mind," I told him. "I must have it mixed up with a creepy van in another abandoned parking lot."

The memory of this snappy comeback kept me happy while I drank a chocolate malt in a booth beside a tinted diner window and watched drunk older kids come blaring in to devour large sandwiches and plates of chili cheese fries. They spilled food on their faces, shirts, and arms while getting most of it into their mouths. It was disappointing that the boy my imagination blessed with charm and intelligence stood up to belch with greater force than he could muster sitting down. Completely unseen, I made my careful exit through a fray of shouting and reckless gestures. It was after three by then, and I felt snug in my sleepiness and invisibility.

At home the lights were on, the ceiling fans spinning, but the rooms were empty, the doors that should have been closed, open. The air felt charged with a panic that made me run around the ground level, looking for someone.

On the patio I found my stepmother, an impressive work of self-made beauty with big pale hair, smoking in her black robe. She stood beneath the moon and gazed out over a mile of dark, shining corn. She'd been asleep and since getting up had poured herself a glass of wine. When I came up to the rail near her, she gasped and took a step back.

"Just me," I said. "No psycho killer."

She squinted down and took a step in my direction. "Your father's looking for you."

I laughed, imagining my father exploring warehouses, deserted docks, shouting my name. He never worried about me and never made me come home by a certain time. "Where is he looking?"

"He just needs to feel like he's doing something." When she was sleepy, speech did not come easily to her, and I took her strange look for effort. "I've been watching him drive around the block for an hour." By "block" she referred to the square mile of cornfield fringed every few hundred yards with houses like ours. Across the field, where the highway joined back road after back road, the twin twinkles of headlights turned in the direction of our road, and disappeared into the dark mass of the crops. "That's him now."

As I looked for his headlights she grabbed hold of my wrist with her cold, hard hand. Something like profound relief came over her. Her grip was strong, and she gazed resolutely into the darkness of the field that lay between us and the sight of my father's headlights. When I tried to pull away she said, "Stay right here with me until he gets here, please." I'd never heard her voice so grim.

I let her hold my hand and stepped closer to her. We were still getting to know each other and, being the girlier of us, she looked almost afraid that I would touch her. Then she hugged me against her and sighed.

"What's happening?"

"Your little friends. Your poor little friends." She could never remember their names, but she could still feel sorry for them. She repeated herself twice and wouldn't say anything more.

The police had discovered Randall's car in a new subdivision where no houses had yet been built, a street making a wide figure eight among undeveloped plots of land. Through the summer the grass had grown tall and seedy, hiding the view of the new street from the country road that led to it, and it was no shocker that Randall and Brianna had been going back there to get it on. They were connoisseurs of discreet sex nooks, the way some couples criticize movies and people they know. Until then I'd believed that doing it in seclusion was an appropriate pastime for a pair of invisible teenagers, but now I felt ashamed of my joke.

The police had been called about teenagers screaming in the subdivision. When they arrived they found only the car and no sign of Randall or Brianna, who evidently still had her purse. People agreed that this was a good sign, though maybe just to agree there was a good sign. Both windows on the driver's side of Randall's car were shattered. But there was no blood in the car or on the street, no further signs of struggle, and so the police were hopeful.

Because the detective considered time was an important factor, he questioned me that night in my living room. Eager to help, I rehearsed describing the van while watching our front window for headlights. When they arrived my father and stepmother left me alone with a youngish, good-looking detective and a couple of policemen. This wasn't the same detective who'd looked for my mother, but his personality made up for the dissimilarity.

Detective Volmar had a scar on his lip and spoke courteously. He sat with his legs crossed and listened as I explained the awful prognostications I'd experienced at Great Skate when I'd seen the van.

"But afterward you let your friends go home," he said at one point. "Why did you do that?"

"I guess I wasn't scared anymore. I should have trusted my instinct. I knew he was an invisible."

The detective had a mean-spirited, doubtful smirk. "An invisible?"

"It's someone who doesn't get noticed, who for one reason or another isn't memorable. I think maybe some of them go bad, become things like kidnappers, or serial killers."

"That's interesting. How do you know this van driver was an invisible?"

I explained how invisibles stand out to one another, how the traffic cop at Great Skate hadn't even seen the strange van, even though it was parked so conspicuously in the seemingly inaccessible old parking lot. Therefore, I reasoned, the van driver was an invisible.

Detective Volmar told one of the cops standing by to find out who this traffic policeman was and to get him on a cell phone or radio. "How did you notice him, then? If he was an invisible."

"Because I'm an invisible," I said. "And my friends are, too. That's how he saw us."

After asking a few more questions Detective Volmar thanked me and said he'd appreciate it if he could question me at a later date, should his investigation require it. I told him I only wanted my friends to turn up.

He laughed, I suppose at my eagerness. "Gosh you're a nice kid, um . . ." He glanced at his report for my name, then admitted with a wince that he'd forgotten it. "Sorry."

"Don't worry. Happens all the time."

The suburb was in an uproar for days. The police department issued a temporary sunset curfew, and in every class at school I sat within earshot of some boy or girl who complained about getting taken into the station or sent home by stern police officers. There were as many stories about sightings of the maroon travel van, near the trailer park, in the oceanic parking lot of the old supermarket, all of them obviously derivative of urban legend. In the halls you saw the usual theater created around a local tragedy.

Outwardly my peers showed sympathy for Randall and Brianna. Many joined hands and wept at the assembly where the principal reminded us that we were one community. Girls who never spoke to me invited me to sit with them at lunch.

I declined, sat in the bleachers by the baseball diamond, as usual, though the absence of my best friends made it impossible to eat anything. The weather was getting colder and windier, the sky higher up, and it was even a little frightening to sit near the empty dugout, so far from the school building that no one would have heard me shouting if I'd needed help. But mostly I felt sad, hoped my friends would turn up, and doubted they would. This struck me as the kind of situation where hoping is something you do to allay dread. Our farming region was small, its people interconnected in a way that made secrets short-lived, and I feared that the driver of the maroon travel van and my friends were long gone.

Once my mother explained that invisibility could be an advantage. "I don't want to fill your head with too many possibilities, little girl." We were sitting on swings at the metropark, her shoes mired in wood chips while mine dangled above them, and she was talking on and on while I adored her — our usual rapprochement. "I don't want other people's inventions to get in the way of your imagination. Who knows what you could come up with? I talk too much to have a good idea, so I sure as hell don't know. You seem like a good apple to me. Am I right? Are you a good apple?"

"I'm a good apple," I insisted.

"I know it, little girl. You don't have to tell me. I don't have to worry about you going off the map and doing something crazy."

Going off the map, she'd said. The idea intrigued me, though at the same time it was a disappointment. Hadn't I been off the map my whole childhood? Wasn't I still off the map, a seventeen-year-old whose idea of a good time on a Friday night was roller-skating in giant circles in a crowd of twelve-year-olds?

No one knew what I thought, and I was little more than a statistic in attendance- and grade-books. English teachers wrote little congratulatory notes on my essays, but I only wrote back to them what they'd said in class. And anyway they were invisibles, too. My father had to work all the time. His parenting style consisted of giving me money and trusting me.

The first time I dreamed of Brianna and Randall after they disappeared, my bed was in the middle of the floor at Great Skate. The rink must have been closed, because the music was off and only a few lights were on. We appeared to be the only people in the place. I had awoken there, still wearing baggy pajamas, to find them skating circles around me. My friends had changed. They spoke and skated like Randall and Brianna but looked older, sickly, their eyes sunk in their faces.

"Hi, Cynthia," said Brianna, whizzing past.

"Hey, Cynth," said Randall, over her shoulder.

"Where have you two been? Everyone's been so afraid for you."

"They shouldn't be," said Brianna.

"No reason to worry about us. None at all."

"You shouldn't keep secrets from your friends," said Brianna, circling again.

"You should have told us we were invisibles, Cynthia," said Randall.

"You knew."

"I didn't think you'd believe me," I said.

"You should have trusted us," said Randall.

"We're your friends."

"We could have gone off the map a long time ago," said Randall. He frowned, shaking his head. "A long time ago. That would have been best for everyone."

"What did you say?"

"Have you ever thought about going off the map?" asked Brianna.

"I definitely prefer life off the map," Randall said. "It's everything I dreamed it would be."

"Or would have, if someone had told us about it."

"Have you seen my mother?"

Brianna's grinning face glided close to mine. There were frown lines around her little mouth. "You want to know where we heard that?"

Randall moved up next to her. His teeth looked gray in the low light. He was pointing off to the side of the rink, to the shadows around the concessions counter. "We heard it from him."

The moment I became aware of the silhouette of a man standing at the edge of the rink, I was possessed by such a desire to scream that I woke up in my bed, back in my bedroom. It was early morning, before seven, and in a few minutes my alarm would go off. Outside, rain fell from a dark sky into the acres of dispirited corn plants.

Though the wait tortured me, I let two weeks pass before investigating the site where Randall and Brianna had vanished. Each night my friends met me in the dark skating rink and cautioned me to wait for the police to leave the crime scene alone. Their faces were getting older. For a few days I stayed home from school and flipped through yearbooks, reexamining pored-over panoramic photos for our faces. In all three yearbooks there were only the standard shots of each of us and, the one year I missed picture day, they hadn't even listed me under *Not Pictured*. Afraid of police by day, afraid of the maroon van by night, I drove around, often taking the road that led past the subdivision where they were heard screaming. I couldn't see over the tall grass that blocked the street inside. I attended unsolicited conferences with the pamphlet-bearing guidance counselor at school and watched television in an empty house.

One morning, just before I woke for school, Brianna and Randall told me the crime scene would be deserted.

"It's safe to go now," said Brianna.

"If you're still interested, that is," said Randall.

The subdivision-to-be was north of the next township, on a farm road with a few old houses perched jauntily along a deep irrigation ditch. The autumn rain had begun to break down the high grasses in the undeveloped lots, but I still had enough cover back there that I didn't mind getting out of my car to walk around. The weather had knocked down the police tape. Clean light poured out of the sky, drying the few leaves that the brisk wind picked up and flew around the new-paved street.

There was evidence of my friends all over the ground, though the police probably couldn't see that. Dried wads of Brianna's green bubble gum lay like moldy little brains all over the pavement. Cigarettes only she could have broken. There were the wrappers from the tacos that Randall ordered in what he deemed practical boxes of six. Walking along the concave gutter, passing out of the crime scene, I came to a kind of midden of used condoms and wrappers, blown dry and brittle through the warrens of tall grass. I wondered how many were scattered through the undergrowth, and was overcome with the sense that this was all that remained of my friends.

"I seen you come in here."

When I looked up I didn't see the old man who had come from across the street to talk to me — I saw the maroon van, idling in front of me, with a tall man beside it. Long, muscley arms hung out of his shirt, and he wore faded, tight jeans. His blonde hair was long and filthy, his skin a burned red, his black eyes bright and dense. Only a few times in my life had my imagination brought something into this world—usually it took me elsewhere. The vision lasted a second, and then I was looking at an old man in bib overalls, standing a few feet away from me. Seeing he'd scared me, he lowered his shoulders and turned slightly. He'd parted his hair on the right, presumably with the comb in his breast pocket.

"Hi," I said.

"You should go home. The police still come around sometimes, and they wouldn't be happy to run into you back here."

"My friends were the ones who . . . were here." I didn't know how to describe what had happened to them to this stranger.

"The ones got taken." The old man nodded. "I called the cops about it."

It was only then that I noticed the blandness in his face, the lights-out quality that rises in a person's eyes after years of being overlooked. "You saw the van, too?"

From the way he puckered his lips as he nodded, it was obvious he felt responsible for my friends' disappearance. "I used to think, 'Let them have their fun back there.' I know things are different now, but I got married when I was about their age. I always thought any kids who had the nerve to go off like that deserved a little time alone." He looked at me hard and said, "Not all of us find somebody who's exactly like us, if you catch my drift."

"I know," I said, remembering how my mother pitied my father for failing to understand her.

"Then I seen him follow them back in here, and I knew I made a mistake letting them have the place." He stood with his hands in the deep pockets of his overalls, staring at the taped-off crime scene, which the wind had broken down into an awkward triangle. "I knew I couldn't help them then. Still I came running back here, and that van almost ran me down."

"Do you think the police will find them?" It was stupid to ask this, because asking him to answer hurt him, more than it did me, watching him struggle to lie.

He gave up and said, "I don't know if I can in good conscience tell you to hope too much."

"I keep dreaming about them," I said.

"I do, too," he said.

Detective Volmar telephoned a few days after I'd visited the subdivision where the driver of the maroon van apprehended my friends. He wanted to know if I was opposed to the idea of a free breakfast. He even offered to come out and pick me up.

"I hate to impose on people in their own homes," he explained a second time, as he drove me through the fields of yellowing cornstalks to the nearby diner where, he couldn't have known, I sometimes ate alone at night. "They get nervous to have a policeman in the house. I guess they're afraid I'll notice the infraction of a tiny law while I'm there, one they don't even know they're breaking. People break laws all the time. Sometimes I think we have so many just so I can arrest someone if I know I need to."

In daylight the restaurant was cleaner and full of shadows, staffed with new cooks and waitresses, strangers to me. We sat down at a booth whose window gave out to a view of the township's main street, the storefronts of old lawyers' offices and a realtor. Detective Volmar said he found all this very quaint. Then he ordered the largest breakfast platter on the menu and requested extra bacon. He drank black coffee in large gulps and knew where his mug was without looking at it.

I ordered a cup of yogurt with granola, something I could crunch on and finish without really trying to eat. Between the weird dreams and missing my friends, my appetite still hadn't returned. The detective may have thought I was a dainty eater, though maybe I flattered myself to think he noticed. He listened to me with interest, but his eyes were a critical compound of belief and disbelief applied to my every statement. He must have been thinking things he didn't say.

"The first time we talked, you didn't mention that your mother went missing a long time ago."

"Sorry," I said.

"Not at all. I'm surprised your dad didn't say anything. The case is still officially open, but nobody's working on it anymore. Whoever had it figured her for a deserter." With one skeptical shrug he won my gratitude and trust. "There's no evidence for that, though."

"Do you think the disappearances are connected?"

Detective Volmar smiled with what compassion he could muster. "There's no reason to think so. But I've been thinking about what you told me the night I interviewed you in your living room. I'm curious about the connection you made between invisibles and serial killers."

"You really believed me about invisibles?"

He drained half his water glass and shrugged. "We'll see. You obviously believe in them."

"It's because I mentioned the van, and the old man did, too. Isn't it?"

He turned his head away slightly. "I'd appreciate it if you didn't talk to a lot of people about the details of the case. The public already knows too much. As it happens, we don't know much more than the guy who called us, and apparently, you know as much as he does." He paused and let the waitress refill his coffee mug, then continued solemnly, with his fingers playing together on the paper placemat. "But I cannot afford not to be open-minded about this. Two kids have disappeared."

"What do you want to know?"

"Well, you say you're invisible. Plainly, you're not. So what exactly do you mean?"

"It's hard to explain," I said. "I'm not sure I fully understand it either. My mother was never that clear about it. But think of it this way. How did you find out about me?"

Detective Volmar looked from the streaked window to me. "Your father called the station and said you were missing. I guess he'd heard about your friends and thought you were with them. Then you got home, and he called to say you were there."

"So the whole time you were coming to my house, you were expecting to question a seventeen-year-old girl, right?"

"Right."

"So maybe that helped you to see me a little more clearly. Maybe, if you knew nothing about me, I could sit right next to you, and you would never have known it. Not because I'm literally invisible, but because I don't connect to other people. Some people just fall through the cracks. But most of us want to be seen, so we make an effort. I'm somebody's daughter, and until a while ago I was somebody's friend. My mother was somebody's daughter, somebody's friend, somebody's wife, and somebody's mother, in that order."

"What does this have to do with murderers?"

"I think some people get themselves noticed by taking revenge."

"Why not get noticed in a more subtle way?" Detective Volmar's toast arrived, and he proceeded to question me as he scooped grape jelly from a plastic tub. "Why not become somebody's husband or wife?"

I thought of my friends and my mother, how much it enraged me to see the sunset curfew lifted the week before and to see life return to normal at the high school. "Because it hurts a lot when someone forgets you," I said. "Taking revenge is one way to make sure no one ever does it again."

There I was, in the dream that had become nightly. I sat up in bed in the middle of the skating rink, watching Brianna and Randall skate around me like a pair of professionals. They'd improved quite a bit, skating so much in my dreams, and they could do things like double axels and land rolling on four wheels. That said about their skating, their bodies looked considerably worse, older, more starved. One of Randall's ears seemed to be coming off, and a sore I hadn't immediately noticed on Brianna's cheek was growing. What fingernails remained were black, and the skin where the others had been was dry, red, and wrinkled.

Their moods grew nastier with their appearances. I didn't say much, mostly just listened to them describe what it was like to drive around in the van with the man who stood at the edge of the rink. He never moved. I'd begun to doubt that he knew we were there.

Sometimes Brianna or Randall would make a teasing reference to my mother, and I would beg them to tell me where she was, what had happened to her. However, my pleading could only last for so long, as I knew a game when it was being played at my expense, and then I would just sit there, my feelings hurt, as they laughed.

"So why didn't you tell your *boyfriend* where we are?" asked Randall.

"She's afraid he'll like me better. Even like this, I'm prettier."

"What's the use?" I asked. "He can't come into my dream and put you in handcuffs. He wouldn't be interested in that stuff. Besides, he knows where you are."

"And where's that?" said Randall, as Brianna turned about to skate backward, with her arms crossed over her small breasts.

"You're in the maroon van. With that guy. Isn't it obvious?"

Brianna smiled knowingly at Randall. "Do you want to know what we see?"

"Forests, mountains, lakes, eagles, coyotes, a comet," Randall counted off his list on the fingers of one hand, starting over whenever he reached his thumb. "A nautilus shell, sharks feeding in a school of silver fish, the White House, rattlesnakes, tarantula eggs, the Grand Canyon, your mother, cottonmouths, a panther."

"Your mother," said Brianna. "We saw your mother."

"When?"

"When!" Randall shouted.

"Where did you see her?" I asked.

"Where!"

Brianna shook her head at me. "Is that really what you want to know? Or would you rather know if she asked about you?"

Her insight left me speechless; yes, this was exactly what I wanted to know. Whether she missed me, thought of me, regretted leaving. Did she plan to come back?

"No, no, no, and no," said Randall, laughing in the villainous way he had beneath the heart-shaped window of the van behind Great Skate the night of his disappearance.

"Stop, Randall," said Brianna, putting her hands on her sides. I couldn't tell if she was serious; as her face deteriorated it conveyed fewer and fewer variations on a lurid scowl. "You don't know when to quit kidding. Honestly, you'll hurt a girl's feelings that way." She looked at me, the gleaming in her dry eyes limitless. "You can see for yourself. If you meet us. Come to Great Skate this weekend," she said. "You'll know where to find us. But don't tell your boyfriend. We'll know about it, and so will he." She nodded at the silhouetted man at the edge of the rink. The lights in the rink came up then, so I could see the line of his mouth, enough to know that he watched us and disapproved.

Sometimes I thought about what I would have been like if I still had a mother, if I'd look, sound, dress, and think like her. If I would love cruelty like she had.

We would play this joke on my father, when he got home from work.

The joke was only good on certain days. I wanted to play it all the time, but my mother knew better. She would stop in my bedroom doorway, interrupting whatever fantasy I had going on. Her toothy smile made me feel like she'd caught me doing something wrong. "Cynthia, should we hide from your father?"

Nodding yes, I would gather up my dolls, as they were necessary props.

"Where should we hide, so he can't see us?"

The pantry worked best. We could watch through a crack in the door as my father walked around the house, his loafers clacking on the wooden floors, his shoulders trying to shrug off his suit jacket. When he shouted our names my mother would hold me against her, covering my mouth with her hand. If I needed to laugh, tell me, I was to bite her.

After a while my father would grew so frustrated that his patience failed, and he would make himself a sandwich. This amused us because he'd never learned to snack properly. After watching him mutter miserably over his approximation of the perfect sandwich my mother had prepared and hidden in the pantry with us, we'd wait until he took a beer out onto the patio. Then, very quietly, we would emerge from hiding, she to make him a plate and fill the sink with sudsy dishwater, I to sit on the tiles at her feet with my dolls. Once we were in our respective swings of wash and play, she would open the window and call to him to come in.

"Where were you?" my father would ask, moving to dump his poor sandwich in the garbage, now that my mother's handiwork awaited him. "I was just in here looking for you."

My mother would wrinkle her eyebrows, and she'd send me a wink when my father wasn't looking. "Why, we were right here the whole time. You walked right past. I don't know why you didn't see us. Sometimes I think you just don't appreciate us."

Night was falling earlier now, and though the maroon van was not in the old parking lot when I arrived at the skating rink, I wasn't completely filled with doubt. If my friends were indeed alive, on the run with the driver of the maroon van, they would need to make an inconspicuous entrance. They were simply waiting for the right moment to appear and send me a signal to join them. I wondered what it would be like, to feel the road passing beneath me, what the van smelled like inside, all the things I would see from the heart-shaped window.

Every Friday in October was Halloween at Great Skate, and that night I waited in a line of fifth- and sixth-grade vampires, witches, he-devils, she-devils, and various other monsters. I had dressed up like the invisible man from the black-and-white movie by wrapping my face in white bandages and wearing sunglasses. I put my hair up in a bun, under a black fedora, and since I was neither a tall nor a large-chested girl, I blended with the younger children.

The heavyset woman in the little ticket booth charged me for a child's admission, an unforeseen bonus that under other circumstances would have thrilled me but now only disoriented me a little. I entered the booming atmosphere of the crowded skating dome, got a locker and put on my skates, then glided around the polished wooden floor to sounds of campy eighties hits. On the white walls of the rink, echelons of colored light spots slowly rotated against the flow of disguised skaters. The deep voice of the deejay, hidden away in his booth, announced specially themed skates. All around me boys and girls coasted together, five and six years younger than me, already oblivious to me. It was fine, that had been my childhood, and for a while I had fun being nobody, soaring along to the music. I could do and think anything, be anyone, the only catch being that I had no one to share it with. That's when I noticed the man watching me from the rail of the rink floor, back behind the bathrooms, near the fire exit.

He was tall and strong-looking, leaning over the rail on his elbows, staring directly at me once I'd noticed him. He'd brushed his long blonde hair behind his ears, revealing his ruddy face. He lifted one hand and waved at me. His attempt to smile only seemed to worsen his mood. A person like that you could never touch, only brush against, and never truly speak with, only at. At this moment I became sure that my friends were dead. I bent my knees and somehow avoided wiping out on the hard, hot floor. I neither waved back nor turned my head abruptly away, but he continued to watch me as I passed him. He would move his face over, as if to push it into my line of vision, and wink at me.

I tried to think of some way I might slip off the rink floor and telephone Detective Volmar without chasing off the man at the rail. I wanted not only to escape him but to see him hauled off by the police. Nothing short of a complete victory would be acceptable. Under my mask I wanted to cry but knew I had to keep moving. As long as I kept skating, I could find a way out, call for help, and do what I could. I skated until the man relaxed and let his hands hang limp over the rink floor, as if to say he would wait on me. Then I skated through a large group of angels and, with that blockade behind me, coasted off the floor at the far end of the rink. I skated out into the lobby, where I found the crabby traffic cop eating a soft pretzel as he peered into a vending machine that flattened pennies and stamped them with winged roller skates.

Once I'd pulled away the bandages and sunglasses he remembered me. Because I was so upset, he hardly needed to hear my story to come running with me around to the back of the rink. It was difficult to run on my skates, but I was afraid of being left behind, isolated in a space where no one could see me, the only kind of space where I'd be vulnerable to the man I'd seen next to the rink. The traffic cop barked into his radio as he ran ahead of me around the corner into the empty back lot. I nearly lost my balance when I saw there was no maroon van waiting for us.

The officer didn't need to think twice. "We've been looking for that van. He's probably driving something else." He pulled open the emergency exit door of the rink and ushered me inside. "Come on. Show me where you saw him."

We hurried into the red light that filled the domed room, and from the rail along the rink scanned a hundred masked faces for the one I'd seen watching me all night. I looked out on the floor, along the tables by the concessions area, among the few arcade games on the far wall. There was no place where the man could have been hiding, not really. The traffic cop dashed into the men's room and then the ladies' room. A group of little girls came running out, then the cop, looking frustrated.

A minute of confusion passed before the rest of the police came running in. The music was stopped and the children were herded off the floor so the cops could search the premises. The situation quickly became humiliating and inexplicable, with a lot of adults scowling, tweeners complaining. The man who'd been watching me was gone. None of the twelve-year-olds questioned remembered seeing him at the rail. A few said they might have seen somebody, but their voices were too eager. Their descriptions contradicted each other.

In all there were eight police cruisers in the parking lot, their lights flashing in the pungent autumn night. Some of the twelve or so officers complained while looking at me, to let me know I'd wasted their time. Detective Volmar showed up in an unmarked white car and was very kind to me. He told a few other cops that they couldn't understand what I'd been through, though I had the feeling that he, too, was irritated. He put me in the back of his car with the door open and told me to put my shoes back on. Then he telephoned my father.

About a year later, the man who became known as the Lake Erie killer was arrested in a small town in southern Michigan, a short drive from our suburb in the cornfields. The police discovered the bones of an estimated thirty-one people in the crawl space beneath his house. Brianna and Randall's clothes were some of the first pieces of evidence found, and a detective said it was only a matter of time before their skulls were identified. Also found in one of three garages built on the killer's sprawling property was the maroon travel van my friends and I had seen outside Great Skate the night they'd disappeared. I saw this after school in a news flash I watched in my living room and saw part of an interview with the killer's mother and then a segment where a serial killer expert compared this killer to others. When the station broadcast footage of the police arresting the man who had murdered my friends, he wasn't anyone I recognized. He was older, around average height, with neat brown hair and glasses. He had soft cheeks, the sort of face I would never imagine hid plans to kill somebody.

My father and stepmother were there with me, waiting for me to speak, to say that this was the guy I'd seen in the rink that night the police had tried to come to my rescue. They wanted to see my fear vanish forever. I only shook my head. What if my mother was one of the bodies they'd found, one of those so decayed it would never be identified? The more I thought about it the more possible it seemed and the more I understood I might still be sick. My face must have betrayed my fear, because my father and stepmother suddenly grew ashamed of themselves.

"Let's get out of here," I said. Soon, I knew, the telephone would be ringing. Randall's parents and Brianna's mother would be calling to speak to me. There was weeping to do, relief to share, and bitterness to acknowledge, and now there was a figure to blame it on. Out the window behind my father and stepmother, the sun rippled in the golden light above the drying, broken stalks of last summer's corn. It was getting cold again, the days shortening. Soon the outdoor businesses would close for the winter.

"How about ice cream?" I said.

By then I'd stopped dreaming about Brianna and Randall in the skating rink. They appeared in my dreams, but in the usual nonsensical places, their faces no longer marbled with decay, but fresh and young, as I had known them. They didn't seem to remember what had happened to them, even when, during a dream set in my front yard, I saw the maroon van drive slowly past us. In the dream it was sunny, there were birds hunting worms in the grass, and I felt no fear after the van had gone. "I've been wanting to ask you two," I said to my friends. "Is the driver of the van the killer or not? Or is he someone else?"

"What driver?" Randall said.

"I don't know any van driver," Brianna said.

On the day the police caught the Lake Erie killer, my father, my stepmother, and I came back from the ice cream stand having licked our fingers clean. The burnt flavor of sugar cones lingered in our mouths, and rather than accept the grim circumstances awaiting us, my father suggested we use the remaining daylight to build a scarecrow in the front yard. He dug a flannel shirt and a pair of brown corduroys from a trunk of old clothes, and I found a pillowcase we could use for a head. In the yard we stuffed these things full of leaves. We posted an old shovel handle in the hard ground and hung the great grotesque doll on it. I'd painted ferocious blue eyes and a stitched red frown for a face, and my father fastened on a gray fedora with safety pins. My stepmother sat on the porch swing, bundled up in a blanket, watching as she sipped hot peppermint tea.

The day turned dark over the bare trees, faster than we'd expected, and by the time we joined my stepmother on the porch swing, with leaf scraps clinging to our hair and sweatshirts, the sun was setting, and a wild wind had sprung up. The trees swayed, noisily rattling their branches together. We sat in a tight row on the wooden seat and watched the scarecrow flail its arms in the dusk, casting dead leaves up at the shuddering boughs of our maples, like a wizard trying to rebuild the summer. Inside the house, the telephone rang and rang. The answering machine kept switching on, and we laughed to hear my father gloomily repeating that we weren't home. Maybe that was a little cruel, hiding just then, but we would make up for it later. We would call those people back, and shout, laugh, cry—produce the sounds that people make when they're together. We owed them that much, out of the empathy we felt, listening to them speak slowly, faithfully putting words into the void of our answering machine, against the chill that grows when a name is said and silence answers.

THE TEA PARTY

He fell in love, briefly, with a younger woman. They met on project and hit it off one morning in the coffee line, making small talk to ward off a panhandler. Turned out they both loved movies. He wrote screenplays in his free time — scenes, really, which he showed no one — and she had been to film school in North Carolina. Now they both traveled around teaching older people how to use auditing software. They passed hours in unfamiliar offices, explaining keystroke combinations to resistant workers and reading about industry advances, and when it was over they escaped, usually to the art cinema or the place that showed pictures by Antonioni and Godard. As the dark theater brightened around them, something changed. She laced her arm through his, he went tight in the throat, and they would say things he blushed to recall later. There were nights in her hotel room, perhaps many, but the affair went no further than that. Maybe it was because he returned to his bed while it was still dark and the halls were empty, and when he saw her back at the office, she wore a fresh mask of makeup and acted like a stranger, not coldly, but like the friendly stranger he had met that morning in the coffee line. Maybe she had never loved him; maybe he scared her. She was twenty-four, he thirty-seven, married, with twin girls who fought over the phone when he called.

He did not know what made her end it, only that he had been preparing to leave his family without telling her. Being with her had dominated his thoughts as he held filthy rails in trains and sat amid the babble in airports and took long morning swims at the YMCA near the hotel. More than anything else, he thought, his wife's pride would be hurt. Cindy had gotten what she wanted from him in their daughters, twins with fiery red hair and a penchant for singing together and losing clothes in the yard. After a while, she might even forgive him. A small, energetic woman who had not been without a network of friends since college, she had been his ally for years, and then she had become a mother and forgotten him. Perhaps it was unfair to put it like that, but he sensed she had lost her interest in being his wife, and he did not hold it against her. They had known each other too long, and the basis of their marriage had been friendship. He now saw the mistake they had made, but there was no taking back lost years and no use in pointing fingers.

He tried to imagine explaining it to Lindsay, the young woman from work. Sometimes he looked at her and thought, She's just a girl, I'm too old, and I'm doing something very wrong here. But other times he saw her deflect another consultant's advance or stand up for herself to their manager, and she seemed more than a match for him. She knew he was married and a father, and she still went to the movies with him and let him put his hand on her waist and climbed on top of him in the stiff hotel bed. Sometimes when he thought about it he was startled by her forwardness. Maybe she was the stronger one. It was in the midst of this bittersweet confusion, as he sat one morning with his laptop deleting e-mails he had barely read, that he finally understood he was in love.

He resolved to tell her. He had to. He owed it to himself, and to Lindsay. In a way, he owed it to his wife. She was getting older, too; she might want to remarry, and there was no denying that finding someone was harder for a woman in her late thirties, even a woman as attractive and charming as Cindy. It was right to give her as much time as possible. And so, armed with this reasoning and the half belief he was doing the right thing, he went to Lindsay's hotel room that evening. He should have called, but he was feeling anxious to see her. She had not been around the office that day, and he had not found an opportunity to ask about her in an unassailably innocuous manner. She had not responded to his e-mails and text messages, but that meant nothing; they were often very busy with clients. She had probably only been working on a different floor, but he was nervous, afraid something was wrong, that she had stopped loving him because of some fatal remark or gesture, and he told himself soon he would know she had a minor cold and all would be fine. He stood at the door to her room, and when he was sure the hall was empty he put his eye to the peephole. He saw the collapsed image of a sunlit room and white curtains, a slender blur standing in the middle. His feeling of relief was instantaneous. He readied himself for whatever mood she might be in and knocked hard enough to sting his knuckles. He felt as if he were being stabbed in the heart over and over. The chain on the other side of the door rattled, the handle flipped down, and the door opened a few inches.

"Can I help you?"

"Lindsay?" he said. He said it even though he knew right away that this woman was not Lindsay, was too old to be Lindsay, was someone Lindsay would never talk to, unless she was some relative from New Jersey who wore costume jewelry, dyed her hair yellow, and rasped. His hopes collapsed before she answered the question.

"No Lindsay here. You sure you got the room number right?"

He was no longer looking at the woman. Three months, he thought. It had only lasted three months. Why had it seemed so much longer? "I'm sorry," he said. "I made a mistake here. Wrong floor."

The woman's eyes shined with pleasure and distrust. "Okay sir. You have a nice evening." She shut the door and from within came the sound of the dead bolt thrown and the security chain reattached.

He did not know what he would do. He had to call home at some point tonight but just now lacked the strength. If he heard his wife's voice, happily surprised and breathless from some task involving the girls, he might break down and confess what had been his mind these past weeks. He must be careful now, when he was feeling desperate, not to blunder and lose everything. He rode the elevator down listening to two younger men excitedly discussing Victoria's Secret models.

The project manager, Rajan, was in the bar, drinking some kind of Scotch. The Sikh signaled from across the room, smiling through his black beard, looking characteristically dignified in his eggshell-colored turban. His easy grace and discretion were both impressive and terrifying. "Let me buy you a drink, Michael," he said. "I bet you could use one. Now that Lindsay is gone."

Taking the stool beside his manager, he gestured to the bartender to bring him whatever Rajan was having. He didn't care what it was, only that he had a drink to hold. "That obvious, I guess," he said. It was not a question. He wondered, feeling more exhausted than afraid, if Cindy knew.

Rajan was watching NFL highlights on the TV above the bar. It was after six, and the tables were taken up by other businesspeople, good-looking men and women smiling tiredly, speaking in loose and rolling cadences, glad for the solace of trendy entrees and a cocktail at the end of another day in a strange city. Rajan chuckled, a light and musical sound. His dark brown eyes looked incredibly young. "No one knows," he said. "She confided in me."

"What happened? Did I scare her?"

Rajan sighed, as if there was nothing he could say that was not obvious to both of them. Then, shaking his head, he flagged down the bartender. "We will need shots," Rajan said. "Something with a big burn. This man is in pain."

That weekend they were holding a party for his daughters. He remembered when he came into the kitchen of the quiet house (the twins were at school, and Cindy's note said she would be shopping until suppertime, and she had promised the girls Chinese and could he please take them), let Seamus lick his palm, and saw a stack of colorful party hats on the counter. Some weeks ago Amber and Ashley had seen a movie in which a cartoon hippo had her animal girlfriends over for tea, and they had begged their mother to give them a real tea party. Cindy had been reluctant at first, not wanting to spoil the girls when she already made such a big fuss over their annual birthday bash, but once she had given her assent she started planning as if the idea had been hers. It appeared this party would be the most impressive to date. In the backyard, around which they had built a high wooden fence to keep out the homeless who still wandered this part of town, a large blue plastic pavilion had been erected over rows of folding tables and chairs. There were two other long tables, one for the catered buffet and the other for flowers, each flanked by tall black speakers. Croquet wickets were configured in a double diamond in the grass, and the wooden trellis in the garden was laced with blue and pink crepe paper. He wondered if that was premature, searching the vast span of vivid blue sky for a sign of rain. There was still no word from Lindsay. It had been almost a week. Maybe, he thought, he had not been in love with her after all. Maybe the job had confused him, fooled him with the illusion of a second life with each new project. He had moved here ten years ago, and driving back from the airport today he had made three wrong turns.

When he checked his messages later there was an e-mail from her. He read it in the living room while Cindy talked on the phone and sipped cab sauv and his daughters lay on the carpet in their pajamas, watching *Cinderella* on television and protesting when Seamus licked himself. Her e-mail was brutally concise, in his view, though he was comforted to see she had not reverted to using a formal address. *Sorry I went without telling you,* the message read. *I guess I'm not ready for something this heavy. I don't know if it should be heavy. Should it be heavy? Maybe I'll see you later —.*

She used a dash to sign off, always had. Before, he had found it charming, but now it was only more evidence that she had always been afraid of revealing true sentiment.

At the party he was distracted, thinking of her e-mail, its tentativeness, its *I guess* and *Maybe* and *I don't know.* What did a girl go out and do, anyway, after typing up a message like that? His suspicions depressed him. He doubted he remained a tempting alternative to younger men. He knew how to screw, but he could not deny that some of his energy had faded, and he could not match the intrigue of young men lurking in the clubs — and, if he was honest with himself, that thrill of being young and going home with someone new did make a difference. One of the caterers was about the right age, early to midtwenties, a wide-shouldered, friendly kid with fashionably shaggy blonde hair who introduced himself as Tristan. Tristan knew his part as the handsome hired help, rolling up the sleeves of his white button-down shirt to show off his forearms and grinning when the little girls turned speechless in his presence, standing straight and aloof while the youngish mothers stole glances at him. Maybe he would know what a girl like Lindsay would do after writing a message like that.

It was his first tea party, truth be told, and he was not sure what to do with himself. He was surprised to see how comfortable the mothers seemed, making it up as they went along, as if tea parties were as commonplace in their lives as margarita night and trips to the mall. He was not sure Avril Lavigne was supposed to be playing. But he said nothing and did as he was told. Like the other adults, he was expected to sit in a small chair at the table with the girls. Amber and Ashley had insisted on assigned seating, and he was placed at the head of the table, where as the only male guest he seemed to play a strictly symbolic role. No one spoke to him as he drank his tea black and ate crackers and salmon pate and salty little sandwiches cut into fours. He accepted three pieces of strawberry cake and listened to the talk swirl around him, much of it rehearsed. Cindy and the other mothers discussed property values since the recession began and how smash-and-grabs were on the rise, but how even with its little crime waves, this historic midtown neighborhood was far superior to the north suburbs. The girls had begun by being polite to each other, saying please and thank you and would you like some more of this or that, but they had grown bored and moved on to comparing phones and Facebook pages. This turn of events had made Amber and Ashley begin to pout, because the twins were not allowed to have phones until middle school, though he doubted Cindy would hold out against the girls' whining until then.

Cindy took note of her daughters' moping, leaned over the table, a dark forelock dangling over her pale forehead, and smiled at him. "Honey," she said, her eyes mildly entreating, "why don't you lead the girls in a game of croquet?"

"Yes, let's play croquet," said Amber, only too happy to cut off the phone talk.

"Daddy's on our team," said Ashley.

"That's not fair," protested a girl down the table. "You'll kill us with him."

"It's our party, so we should be able to win," Amber said.

"Nuh-uh," said the girl with the impressive phone. "You're supposed to let your guests win."

"Daddy, who's allowed to win?" Ashley said. "Mommy?"

"Girls," said Cindy in her instructive voice. "No one has the right to win. That's why it's a game. The hosts have to be polite and let the guests go first, but they can still win. In fact, they should try to win. To let someone else win is considered rude."

A few mothers nodded to confirm this.

The brunette child pointed her phone at him. "But the teams aren't fair."

Cindy glanced over at Tristan standing at attention, shoulders back, by the chafing dishes on the buffet table. "I bet that if you ask that young man over there, he'd be happy to play with you."

"Oh," said the girl, "we want him on our team."

He could see his daughters were disappointed by this turn of events. They looked on, mouths hanging slightly open in envy and shock at their mother's treachery, as the girl put down her phone and went over to ask Tristan.

Ashley looked down the table at him, her expression fully reflecting his newfound inadequacy. "We're not going to lose, are we, Daddy?"

"No, sweetheart, we're not going to lose." He stood, smiling grimly at Cindy and the other women as he rose and put his napkin on the table. They watched him with amusement and approval, and Cindy mouthed *Thank you.* It struck him as perverse that parenthood should reverse the order of who played along with whom.

He went out to the first stake, where the girls were deciding the playing order, and picked up a mallet and turned it so the sun shone in the finish of its wooden head. Tristan came over looking smug. "It's been a while since I've played this, man."

"Me, too."

The younger man looked at the two teams of girls and back

at him. "I bet this isn't how you'd prefer to be spending your afternoon."

"No, I guess not. But there are worse things."

Tristan gave a skeptical frown. "Like what?"

He looked at the young man's catering outfit. "Well, how do you like working Saturdays?"

"It's all right." Tristan shrugged, untroubled by his predicament. "My friends aren't really getting into anything cool until later, so it's no biggie. Plus it's pretty sweet to see what these houses look like on the inside." He glanced back at the women watching them from the pavilion. "Plus," he confided, "there are other perks. If you know what I mean."

He felt his ears growing hot. Not that he doubted that what Tristan said was true—he felt certain, with a measure of horror and fascination, that it was. But it annoyed him that this kid thought the comment would fill him with admiration and curiosity, and it disturbed him further that it had. He was taller than the caterer, and he looked down at him with open contempt. He wasn't afraid to tell him to get off of his property, put this kid in a position where he would have to explain himself to his employer. "What perks? Do you mean playing croquet with little girls?"

Tristan blushed. "Never mind, dude."

"No, seriously," he said loudly. "Why don't you list out the unusual perks of your job?" He glanced over at Cindy, who looked confused and grinned seeking reassurance that all was well.

The caterer turned and shrugged. "Let's just play this, man. Whatever. Look, it's your tea party."

"Damn straight." He said it louder than he'd intended, and the girls were staring now. "Come on," he said, with maybe a little too much force. "Let's play."

He got off to a strong start. He knocked the blue ball through four wickets on his first turn and then, nodding as his wife and daughters gave him faint applause, settled back with his hands stacked on the mallet handle to watch Tristan. The caterer took to playing with intense concentration on what he was doing. His cheeks were still flushed with color, and he kept his head bent, his small bright eyes focused on the red ball he was hitting. On his third stroke he swung the mallet and popped the ball through the wicket and into Michael's ball, knocking it out of bounds into the gravel by the sliding glass door. The girls on his team applauded, as did some of the mothers in the pavilion. With a look of satisfaction on his face, Tristan lined up his next shot, seemed to consider what to do, and then hit the ball just short of the next wicket. He glanced up and smiled quickly, as if to say he had done it on purpose.

He watched the next two rounds in a barely contained rage. As soon as his ball was live again, he resolved to first make the next wicket and then to croquet Tristan's ball as far off the course as he could. His shoulders trembled as he took his next shot, knocking the ball further than he'd intended, but striking the caterer's ball just the same and sending it off toward the garden and out of bounds.

"Nice shot!" Tristan said.

He ignored this, as well as Cindy's cheering in the tent and the clapping of his daughters behind him. He went to his ball and lined up his next stroke, aware in his periphery of Tristan's broad grin. It was his turn to put his head down. He concentrated on making the next two wickets. From here, he knew, he would be far enough ahead that Tristan wouldn't catch him, and he would give the girls the lead which, for them, evened the field against girls who had phones.

He talked to her later that day, but the conversation felt unnatural. He was the one who called. He knew the gesture would not help his cause, that phoning signaled he assumed it was over and demanded an explanation. He did it anyway. He knew it was selfish. If he had been younger, he might have said he couldn't resist, but now he knew better, that he was indulging himself by asking for what she must feel she owed him, even if that was all they had left.

He stood on the sidewalk in front of the black wrought iron fence. The caterers were packing up their white van, and up and down the street, trees were growing pale buds. The crocuses in the garden had already opened white and purple flowers. The spring was coming on relentlessly this year, an all-encompassing storm of pollen and light.

Her phone rang three, four, five times. His heart sank as he decided against leaving a message. But then she answered.

"Hey," she said in the tiny voice she used to show fear.

"Hey," he said, unable to disguise his pathetic hopefulness.

She was silent, waiting for him to speak, breathing loudly through her nose.

"I got your e-mail."

"I'm glad," she said.

"Are you sure about what you wrote? Are you sure about not being sure?" He said this with the smile that would have gone with the question, had she been there. He was grateful now as she laughed.

"Yeah, I'm sure. I'm sure I'm not sure."

The caterers were coming out now, carrying the chafing dishes. He wheeled away from them and walked down the uneven pavement until he was in front of the neighbor's white brick house. They had hung their hummingbird feeder, a bright red cylinder, beside their front porch.

His breath felt thick, like syrup in his throat and nose. He had not spoken the way he was about to speak in a long time. He felt like a college boy again, like an amateur. "You know," he was saying, "I have very strong feelings for you, Lindsay. I really, really do."

"I know," she said, like she was cringing, wherever she was.

"I won't tell you if you don't want me to."

"Don't."

He'd known it beforehand, he thought, feeling the tears well up. He walked farther down the street. At the end of the block two homeless men sat on a low wall at the corner drinking from bagged pint bottles. They leered at him, and he glared back, outraged that they should see him like this. He closed his eyes and asked the question he knew he should not. It came welling up out of him like laughter. "You feel differently?"

"Oh God, Michael." She sounded miserable. At least there was that. "You know I don't want to be victimized by my past, right?"

He was confused. The feeling of her words was all wrong to him. He swallowed and his breathing slowed. "Wait. What are you talking about?"

"You know. You remember. All that stuff with my father? How he ran out on my mom and me?"

"Oh, yeah," he said flatly. He had known that about her biography, but he had not seen their situation parallel to it. He stood frozen in surprise, his tears sliding back, falling into his throat where he could swallow them. He felt suddenly embarrassed to be talking to her, eager for the conversation to be over. He thought of the number of people who knew about them, Rajan, others she must have told. He would have to carry on now as if it had never happened.

"I just don't want to be that woman," she went on. "I don't want to go after married guys because it's safer, you know? I just don't want to be a victim."

"I see," he said flatly, unable to hide his disappointment. Really, he had expected more from her than such a sordid little fantasy.

He wondered if he had ever been on the same date with her, or if he had always been alone at the movies, sitting with a stranger in a friendly looking disguise. She was in the middle of saying something, but he cut her off. "Look, I should go. We're wrapping up my daughters' party."

There was a violent intake of breath on the other end. "Michael, don't be like that."

"Maybe I'll see you later." He touched the End button before she could say more. He turned and saw Tristan coming up the sidewalk, smiling at him. The younger man had spilled a little soup on the front of his shirt, and it had stained yellow. Aware of his swollen eyes, wondering if he looked as if he had been crying, he gulped and mustered a big smile to match the freshness of his voice. "Hey Tristan. You guys about finished up?"

"Yes sir. You know, Mister —"

"My name's Michael."

"I just wanted to say I was sorry for what I said to you during the game. It was really inappropriate, and I hope there are no hard feelings." He held out his strong right hand, its skin still uncreased and tight. "I totally didn't mean to disrespect your house."

He accepted the handshake and dropped his chin ironically to show the gesture was unnecessary, because there was no problem, never had been. "Don't worry about it, Tristan. I wasn't really angry at you anyway." He reached into his pocket and brought out his wallet. Shaking his head when the caterer held up a hand, he pulled out four twenties and gave them to him. "Here's a tip for each of you. You going out tonight?"

Tristan was still looking at the bills, holding them tight in his hand. "Um, yeah. I'm going to the Highlands."

"Have one for me," he said.

Tristan squinted in happy confusion, then looked back at the van, where the other caterers were climbing in. "Definitely, man.

I definitely will." Beginning to blush under the attention he was getting, he looked back at the door they had left open and mumbled, "Well I better go. I guess we're going now. Thank you, sir. It's really generous."

"Call me Michael," he said. "That's my name."

But the caterer was already halfway down the sidewalk, running as though his coworkers might depart without him. When he reached the open door, he hopped into the backseat and, without looking back, pulled on the handle behind him. The door slid shut with a firm bang. The driver pulled the front end away from the curb, and a moment later the white van was racing with a faint bounce up the street.

The block lay quiet, its trees in gentle motion. A golden dusk was descending. He looked up the sidewalk, mentally retracing his steps, passing through the gate, and reentering his lavish house. Inside, his absence would have gone unremarked. The mothers were gathering their daughters, who were begging to stay overnight. Cindy was in the kitchen handing out goody bags, and the twins were plotting to extend the party. The night lay ahead, and he could do as he pleased. Tomorrow meant getting on another airplane, checking into another hotel. That part would be easy. This past January, curious, he had performed a rough count, and found he had done it more than a thousand times.

WHITEOUT

Now the snow poured down so Mason only glimpsed the road between wiper flaps. On the windows the snow built to ridges and fell away, and when he looked out seeking a familiar glimpse of flat, snowbound farmland, there were only individual flakes whipped out of a slurry of descending whiteness. He'd been alone on the road for almost an hour, a privacy he'd used to cry about Wendy at first, though the grief had passed, giving way to a feeling of giddy excitement. He was going home for the first time in thirteen years.

The freeway was closed, and there had been no patrol cars since the announcement, back before the radio voices turned mushy. He doubted he would see one before he reached Mansfield. It was Christmas Eve, and the slashed state budget meant fewer cops all over.

A deejay had described the storm stretching from the Canadian Rockies to the Appalachians, dumping snow on central Ohio until tomorrow afternoon, delivering more white than anyone wanted for Christmas. Mason had laughed. Like a snow globe, the pun contained the entire Midwest. He opened the ashtray and got out the baggie of crushed cocaine. He had it tied off with a twister around a red cocktail straw for easy access while driving, and he took a snort, never taking his eyes from the vanishing and reappearing road, careful to miss nothing.

It was four o'clock and growing dark. In his parents' house the furnace bellowed in the basement. His older brother was opening dessert wine and his mother dusting the cookies with powdered sugar while his father stood by the tree at the living-room window, gazing out on the weather with the military sternness that was his mainmast. That was how it had been thirteen years ago when Mason returned from college at about this hour. He had come in lugging a bag of dirty laundry, prepared to deliver a rehearsed speech about how he'd failed out his first semester. He was not ready to see his mother so happy, wiping her hands on her apron so she could take him by the ears and kiss his forehead and cheeks, or Leonard waiting behind her with a second glass of port, or his father drifting in, a smile breaking through his solemn features. All that week Mason was unable to tell them, and afterward he'd driven back to school and worked in the tire shop, avoiding their calls until he found a job at a resort in Kentucky and started making his way south. No doubt they came looking for him, found the empty apartment they'd been renting. He might have been in Memphis then. It was hard to say, it was so long ago he felt more embarrassment now than guilt — he had been a boy then. Eventually he'd reached New Orleans and called that home, though these last few years, when he was feeling especially rotten and desolate, he'd taken to monitoring his family on the Internet. He thought about calling sometimes, but it felt like a lame gesture, and he was more interested in them, anyway, than in telling the story he sensed they'd want to hear about him.

Tracking them was easy, given his brother's tendency to post family news on his blog, even though no one posted comments save for the occasional fat cousin from Michigan whom nobody saw. Mason had been watching them for some time now. He knew all about them, felt as if their lives had been restricted to a small compartment of his consciousness. Sometimes he felt he might be connected to them in a way modern science couldn't explain. He knew details, his father's heart congestion, his mother's struggle with her bone density. He knew Leonard had lucked into a managerial position at Toyota and was seeing a woman who had a little girl. He had seen pictures online—the woman, Tanya, was good looking, surprisingly so, given Leonard's characteristic dullness and expanding paunch, and the daughter, a blonde child with gapped front teeth, was exceptionally cute. He felt he knew Tanya and her daughter intimately, though he'd never met them, and though people in his hometown frowned on mystical thinking, he sensed that if he kept his mouth shut when he met them they would find themselves mysteriously charmed by him. They had been planning for some time to go to his parents' today and open presents, and Leonard had mentioned it so many times on the blog that Mason wondered whether his brother wasn't really posting secret messages to him. Of course Leonard would never do this consciously; he was too jealous, too attuned to his local frequencies. But maybe some part of him, something spiritual, reached out to Mason while the dumb body labored on. He imagined Tanya's daughter shrieking with delight as he threw her into the air and caught her repeatedly, while Tanya and his parents looked on, amazed by his way with kids, and Leonard unable to conceal his envy. It was not too late, he thought, never too late for family, for even if he had been the troublemaker, he had always been the favorite. Long before his troubles began, he saw himself in the story of the prodigal son. He was the carrier of his family's joy. He reached for the baggie in the ashtray.

They were going to be so surprised. Maybe too surprised. Maybe he should call from his cell phone to diminish the shock of his arrival. There was his father's heart to think about. His mother's ticker probably wasn't shipshape either. He picked up his phone and nearly called, but then he remembered he was driving in extremely hazardous conditions, and then he remembered his earlier reasoning that it would be better to wait until he had stopped the vehicle before he broke a thirteen-year silence. A shiver of pleasure ran from his throbbing head down through his spine and arms and butt. It was a good thing he wasn't any higher.

He glimpsed a passing exit leading up to what must have been a country highway. This couldn't be Mansfield, not yet, and even if he wanted to stop to rest, there was nothing out here but farmhouses and barns and silos scattered over vast tracts of snowy farmland, and if you had asked Mason to guess how many of those structures had been abandoned for decades he would wager more than half, the rest inhabited by couples of a vanishing generation, people so old they were probably already tucking themselves in for the night.

He had to push on another couple of hours at this slow-going speed, which with the coke would be no problem. He would slow and make the gradual turn into his parents' driveway, and the people inside would see the headlights. He had presents, a backseat filled with them, gift-wrapped in shining silvery blue paper and red ribbons this very morning at a mall in northern Kentucky. Shopping had been a revelatory experience. Wandering among the stores, he had been seized by a spirit of generosity and serendipity that felt new to him. He found himself spending twice what he had vaguely budgeted, but it didn't matter; he could always pour more drinks, and people would give him money. That had always been simple enough. He found he had a talent for choosing the right gifts. There was a book on history's greatest military campaigns for his father, a copper-clad sugar boiler for his mother, a new bass fishing rod for Leonard. Though he had yet to meet Tanya, he was sure he knew her better than his brother did, reading beyond the observations in Leonard's blog, and he had picked out a sleek leather jacket for her, figuring her for a size six—if he was wrong, there was always the gift receipt. For the little girl, he had picked his favorite board game, The Game of Life, in which you started out with a single plastic peg representing a person and rolled dice to advance along squares in a road on a cartoon landscape while acquiring a car, an education, a job, a family, and a fortune. While you could choose certain things, like whether you wanted to retire, your ability to do what you wanted depended on luck, the roll of the dice, the card of fate. It was just like real life, Mason thought as he reached for the baggie in the ashtray, except it only lasted an hour or so, and you could play as many times as you wanted, be as many people as you wanted, and there were no real consequences to what you did. Which wasn't like real life, contrary to what the salesman in the toy store entrance had tried telling him.

Just thinking about it made Mason furious all over again.

The guy was from India or Bangladesh or someplace like that, this salesman whose eyes had sought Mason's from across the store filled with children, tired parents, noisy video games, and mechanized singing teddy bears. He was in his late forties, his face clean shaven, his black hair turning white around his ears. He beckoned for Mason to come to the folding table he'd set up in the doorway of the shop. He was sitting in front of a steel box with a meter divided into fields of blue and red. The meter's red plastic arrow rested just to the left of the zero in the blue field.

"How are you, sir?" the man asked in a solemn unaccented voice, as if they had embarked on a costly business transaction. "Enjoying your shopping?"

"Merry Christmas." It occurred to Mason the guy might not celebrate the holiday, but then what the hell did he expect, selling whatever he sold in a mall the day before Christmas? He set down his clutch of plastic bags and put his hands on his hips. He was feeling the need to duck into a bathroom and get the baggie out of his coat's inner pocket. After he learned about this steel box. "This looks like a Geiger counter or something. What's it measure?"

"Stress," the man told him.

Mason laughed. New Age shit—he should have known. "How does it do that exactly?"

The man stood and offered him two small steel rods with steel buttons on their top ends. The rods were connected by wires to the Geiger counter thing. "Take a wand in each hand and let it rest there. When you are ready, rest your thumbs on the indicators on the top of each wand. The meter will determine your stress level and show us with the indicator arrow."

The rods were the weight of supper knives. Mason felt doubtful holding them, pressured to buy something. He wished he had refused to hold them. "These are going to measure my stress?"

"Yes. Rest your thumbs on the indicators when you are ready."

Mason felt nervous. The things were probably rigged so that your stress reading was through the roof. The man regarded him with the detachment of someone confident of his superiority. He was probably selling herbal remedies or something. Mason put his thumbs on the steel buttons and looked down at the stress meter. The red arrow swung rapidly through the blue field and into the rightmost quadrant of the red field and wavered there at a spot between the numbers seventeen and eighteen. Great, he was probably about to have a heart attack right here.

"What the fuck does this mean?"

The man took the wands. "It means you have a great deal of stress in your life."

He thought of Wendy again and felt the clamp of guilt. He was getting irritated with this stranger. It was none of his business. The certainty in the man's voice disgusted him. "How the fuck does this machine know?"

"You carry the stress in your muscles. It stores up in your nervous system and affects everything you do. The process is unconscious, and it determines how you hold your body and a whole host of things, including how healthy you feel."

"That's a load of shit," Mason said. "Let's see you press the buttons."

The man blinked once, casually accepting the challenge, and placed his thumbs on the buttons. The arrow moved past zero into the second quadrant of the blue field. "Do you see? Six point eight? That is a very healthy level of stress."

"According to whom?"

"Dr. Hubbard has written a book that explains it all." The man brought a thick black paperback with the title *Dianetics* from behind the stress meter. "It is all in here."

It was rigged somehow. Mason looked down to see if some kind of foot pedal controlled the stress meter and saw only the guy's brown loafers against the mall's drab green carpeting. "What the fuck do these numbers even mean? This shit isn't real medicine; it's all made up!"

"Sir, you seem to be aware of your stress," the man said coolly. "There must be things in your life that make you feel strain, things and people. You could cut these out."

It had been a while since Mason felt like he could punch someone. He folded his arms to hide his shaking hands. His heart, beating fast, felt sick to its stomach. "What do you know about me?"

"You could one day live stress free," the man said. "Think about it. You would feel weightless, happier than you have ever been. It would be better for you."

"Fuck you," Mason told the man. "You don't know a fucking thing."

He had grabbed his bags then and gone straight to the nearest men's room stall for two quick snorts from the baggie and then had hurried out to the mall parking lot, where the snow was really starting to come down. The coke helped him feel better, and he convinced himself that he should be proud of his response to this unpredictable nuisance. But as he crossed the border into his home state, he began to doubt that his words had made any impact on the salesman, who had been so sure of himself.

"Motherfucking asshole," he said, clearly envisioning the calm brown eyes floating in the man's impassive brown face, then checking to ensure he was still on the road. "Fuck you, mother-fucker!"

When he came to the overturned minivan, the snow flowed down so heavily that he almost didn't see it lying in the right lane. Its red color helped it stand out it in the light of his headlights reflecting off the falling snow. It was past five now, and he had been traveling at just under thirty miles an hour, and he reckoned he had another thirty miles to go. There was nothing out here but farms and a few small stands of trees. He braked slowly until he was hardly rolling and steered his car to a stop near the shoulder. It seemed more likely that he would be stuck in the snow than that another vehicle would come along and hit his car. He switched on the hazards before getting out.

Wind rose loudly along the dark road, blowing snow across settled snow and against steel dividers with a sound like tinkling glass particles. Snow fell in his hair and on his face as he trudged through the slush on the highway. A whirling gust packed snow under his chin and down his collar. Soon it would be too cold for the salt on the roads to work. He shouldn't wait out here until help came, and anyway he was too deranged from coke and sleeplessness to talk to cops. Still he had better make sure someone was coming. He grew nervous as he approached the dark hulk of the minivan, glancing back to see his car's hazards, tiny red lights blinking in the rippling gray quilt of snow.

He went to the front end of the van and knelt in the cold snow by the window, which was mostly broken out, and turned on the penlight on his keychain. The thin light revealed a plaid, blue blanket with a tousled lock of white hair sticking out from under one end. The person underneath shuddered. "Jim? Is that you?" She sounded tired and cold. He wondered if she could move, if the van was at risk for combustion flipped over as it was.

"No, I'm Mason," he said. "But it's okay. I'm here to help. Is Jim your husband?"

After a few strained breaths she said, "He went for help. To find us a phone."

"I have a phone," he said. "I'm going to call 911 right now. Are you hurt?"

"My shoulder hurts," the woman said. "Where's Jim?"

"Hold on," he said. "Let me call them. I'll go find him."

"Get Jim," she said. "Tell him to come back here. It's not safe to be running around out there. He's not a kid anymore."

He walked away from the van to make the call, covering his phone with his free hand to protect it from the snow. He was afraid there would be no connection, but the signal patched through on the first try. A man answered, his voice flat, and Mason wondered whether it sounded different tonight from any other night, heavier, more resentful. Probably not. He'd heard the holidays were an especially violent and sad time of year for many people. Until recently, he had been one of them. He explained what he had discovered on the highway.

The operator wasn't sure how long it would take for the ambulance to arrive. "I'd be able to guess better if I knew exactly where you were. At least you're on 77. Forty minutes? Maybe sooner. It's pretty bad out there."

"That's too long," Mason said. "The man with this lady, he went off looking for a phone. He's got to be lost in all this snow."

"Just stay with the woman," the operator said. "Back your car up to the minivan and wait with her."

"I don't know," Mason said. "The minivan's upside down. Couldn't it catch on fire? Shouldn't I get her out of there?"

"Sir, I recommend you leave her where she is. She may have a back injury. If there's not a fire yet, maybe there won't be. But now that you mention it, you might want to keep a distance from the vehicle."

"Is that your advice?" Mason couldn't believe what he was hearing. A 911 operator should know exactly what to do.

"It's really up to you, sir. The police are on their way. Just sit tight."

He went back to the window of the overturned van and shined his light on the woman under the blanket. She was shivering, and it sounded like she was crying. "Is that you, Jim?"

"No, it's Mason again. I just called for an ambulance."

"Thank heavens. How long did they say?"

"They said soon," he said. "They're coming as fast as they can."

"Where's Jim? Someone's got to get him before he gets too far," she said. "Someone's got to tell him he doesn't need to call."

"Okay," Mason said. "Okay. What about you? Are you going to be okay here?"

"I'm fine," the woman said. "Go find Jim for me."

"Okay, I'm going." He wished he had another light to give to her, to keep her company. He would have given her his keys with the penlight, but it would be suicidal to leave the highway without any way of seeing his tracks. He rose from the window and took a few steps onto the road, astonished by how quickly the snow covered her presence and he felt alone again. He could walk out into the snow, stand right next to the old man, and never see him. He shined his light along the shoulder until he found a pair of half-filled footprints leading down into the shallow ditch beside the road and up the far side to a snow-filed space that was probably an open field. He hesitated, the edges of his feet already going numb. What if the old guy had already fallen or sat down out there, had given up? What if he'd already died? It would be much easier to stay here on the road and wait for the police. It would be even easier to walk down to his car, get in, and drive away. No one could fault him for that. He had already done a great deal here, perhaps saved the life of the woman in the minivan. Those people shouldn't have been on the road tonight; they were lucky he even came along. He thought of the man with the stress meter telling him how easy his life could be if he abandoned his obligations to others. He thought of his parents, of Leonard and Tanya and the kid listening to his hero story, how hollow it would sound if he never told them how he ran away at the last minute. Or what a terrible secret it would be if he never told them at all. Letting out a self-pitying sigh he stepped down into the deep snow of the ditch.

In early November he had come in around dawn and found Wendy. He was tired from working a double, he later told the police, which made it hard to remember details, but the truth was that he had stuck around after the bar was clean with a cool new guy, doing shots and telling stories, making brief retreats to the bathroom to make use of his baggie. The sun was coming up over the low slanted roofs of Burgundy Street when he found his townhouse's front door unlocked and became angry enough to wake Wendy and lecture her about protecting herself and their things.

Only afterward did he notice the disaster area of the shotgun house's front room and kitchen, the takeout containers lying open on the countertop and table, the empty bottles and ashtrays everywhere, couch pillows lying on the floor. It was if they had been living in a crime scene all along.

Since kissing him good-bye at midnight, she had apparently had quite an adventure, bringing any number of people back to the house. She'd even left the little sliding mirror from the medicine cabinet out on the coffee table with powder smudges on top. He went to the bedroom and found the bedclothes in the usual tangle. He tried to stay calm then, telling himself she'd gone back out, was possibly opening another beer right now in one of their friend's living rooms, so blitzed she'd never recall leaving the door unlocked. He was already on his way into the bathroom, pushing open the door, seeing the water on the tiles.

She had been packed into the bathtub fully dressed. Her dirty feet hung over the edge. Someone had tucked her elbows in at her sides, tilted her head back under the faucet. Her hazel eyes looked up emptily. Her clothes and hair were soaked, her pallid face rinsed with water, looking almost clean and innocent but for the marks on her cheeks where someone — a man, he first assumed then and simply came to believe afterward — had slapped her repeatedly to wake her up.

He kept walking long after he could no longer make out Jim's tracks in the snow. He was chilled through the bones of his feet and hands, and his teeth were chattering in his ears. His clothes were all wrong for this mission. By now the paramedics and police had surely reached the scene of the accident, and things were under control. Maybe Jim was back by now, too, standing among the uniformed men, soberly speculating about where the well-meaning, if foolish, Samaritan had gone. He didn't believe this version of things; it was too tidy. He was going to die out here, and so was Jim. They both were going to die out here. So much for the prodigal son, he thought, though something in him refused to accept it.

He reached for the baggie of coke he had transferred to his coat pocket and ran up against a man standing upright in the field. Small but sturdy, the man stood turned away from him, bundled tightly in his old trench coat and hunching against the cold, with tiny drifts of snow piled up on the brim of his fedora. Mason touched his shoulder. "Jim?" he said. He laughed morbidly. "I've been looking all over for you."

When the man didn't respond, Mason tried turning him by the shoulder. Something under the coat was hard and bulky. He reached out to take the hat, and the head rolled back, revealing the black stitchwork connecting the head to the burlap sack body. The face under the frayed hat brim was featureless sackcloth, frozen stiff and stained with dirt. A wind came up and one of the scarecrow's arms flew around, throwing flecks of ice against his cheeks, and Mason let go to cover his face with his unfeeling hands.

He stumbled forward and saw something large and dark looming ahead, a mass to which the falling snow conformed. He hurried forward, getting closer, fighting through a drift to his thighs, until he came up against the frozen wood of a barn wall. As a boy he used to look at them from the backseat of his father's car, half curious about these relics of the cornbelt days, so many of which had been used as billboards for chewing tobacco. He had never been this close to one. Holding his hand against the icy grain of the wood, he made his way around the structure, hoping to find a house on the other side.

The farmhouse stood in a ring of naked maple trees whose branches were thrashing in the wind. The dark shapes of cars stood in the driveway. A light was on inside, within the front door. He hurried through the snow, falling once, and used the iron railing to pull himself up the front steps. Exhaustion and drug withdrawal were catching up with him. He did not know what he would say when he began to ring the glowing, orange doorbell, which he pressed over and over. After a while, a man opened the inner door and looked out.

It was almost ten when he finally called his parents. He was sitting in the kitchen of the farmhouse, the presents he had picked out for his family laid out on the table before him. The couple who lived there had been very kind, giving him dry clothes to wear and offering to let him stay the night in one of the spare rooms upstairs. After talking with the local sheriff, the farmer had taken Mason in his truck with a snowplow to retrieve his car, which was now parked in the driveway, behind the sedan that belonged to the couple's son and his wife. Mason had talked to the police, who seemed to take his state of mind for confusion and panic and cold. They too had been kind, thanking him for his help. They had found Jim on the freeway, wandering in the wrong direction, confused and upset. He had mild frostbite on some of his fingers and his nose, but he was otherwise okay. By now he and his wife were at a hospital somewhere.

The farmer was a serious man with a strong air of religiosity, and in the course of taking Mason back to his car and offering to put him up he had repeatedly and pointedly made references to God, to whom he clearly felt Mason owed his life. The farmer was courteous but also wary and faintly disapproving, having detected something he didn't like in his unforeseen guest. Now that he had fulfilled his obligations as host, he had left Mason in the kitchen and gone back to the living room, where his grandchildren were up past their bedtimes, opening presents. From the archway to the brightly lighted room came the sounds of paper tearing and the chirpy voices of small children, the reluctant admonishments of moderately drunken parents.

Mason sipped hot tea from a mug, which announced in cartoon font, *The Early Bird Gets the Worm!*, and depicted a smiling bluebird in a nobleman's blouse uprooting a pale worm from the ground. He wanted another bump from the baggie in his coat, but he thought he'd let it wait until he was off the phone.

His brother answered. There was a pause in the space after Mason spoke his name. Leonard said something to people in the background, and suddenly he heard his father and his mother speaking to him. A little girl asking a question and being told to hush. That would be Tanya's daughter. They had him on speaker phone and were trying to take turns talking to him. His father went first, in a voice steady and calm, almost subdued. His mother, too, sounded so careful. To hear their caution made him wince, but he answered their questions as best he could. The connection was poor. He listened to their voices, trying to see their faces through their tones. After a long silence on Mason's end, his father remarked that the call had been dropped, and they should hang up and wait for him to call back.

"Wait," he said, in a voice that sounded desperate to him. He said he was there, though it had already dawned on him that it would be tomorrow before he could prove it to them. He said a few things about the severity of the storm, then promised to tell them his story in the morning. When he hung up, he knew by the sound of their voices that they had not believed him completely. It was not disbelief he had heard, or even skepticism, but an awareness of who he had always been.

He carried the presents up to the guest room as quietly as he could, hoping the groans of the steps beneath him blended into the storm. He was looking forward to another snort, but then he changed his mind, thinking instead to pass out and take the shortcut to the morning. The air in the room smelled like mothballs, and a layer of cold air drifted over the floorboards. He did not bother to turn on the light. The window was dark, crusted with a layer of snow, visible only by the faint violet light outside. He climbed into the bed fully clothed, pulled the quilt to his chin, and gazed at the dark ceiling above. The mattress was narrow and lumpy, and all he could do was lie there and wait for sleep. He thought of Wendy again, and in the painful instant that followed it seemed that it was, this feeling he had run from thirteen years ago, the fear of the way life unfolded in this place, with slow and unflinching inevitability. He opened his eyes and saw the presents lying in a neat stack beside the bed, their wrappings gleaming faintly. After a moment, he remembered what each contained but could not say why he had chosen them. He let out a sigh and felt his body start to relax. Sleep was closer than he had imagined. Tomorrow he would drive home and see his family. Whatever happened after that, happened.

HENRIK THE VIKING

Six weeks, seven. Perhaps one-third of women experienced light bleeding or spotting during the first trimester. About thirty percent of them miscarried. This last fact should not scare them, Dr. Kornblum elaborated in her California monotone, but give them hope: consider the 70 percent who got their babies. The odds were with them. Who knew where this blood came from? The body was a mystery, an ancient adventurer. Without brazen biology, none of them would be there in the clinic, listening as computer speakers amplified the whisper sound of the baby's heartbeat.

Hazel had read this much on the Internet, and she milked the sound of the words until she realized Kornblum and Riley were waiting for her to speak. She being the pregnant one and all. She looked into their eyes and announced that she was feeling uncharacteristically brave. "I thought all the stuff I read was written by crazy people on the Internet," she said. "But maybe some of it was by sane people on the Internet."

Riley nodded energetically and declared that he agreed with the women, and then he rubbed and massaged the knots in Hazel's back for a long, quiet time.

That evening they called their parents and told them to expect to become grandparents in the spring. Hazel's parents opened a bottle of wine and stayed on the line until well after they were drunk and talking seriously about heading out to a bar. Riley's parents, lower-intensity people, conveyed their blessings after a round of happy sniffles. When it was over Hazel and Riley set their cell phones aside to charge and opened the windows to let in cool night air. On the street, strangers called out to each other in drunken voices. Above the streetlights and the airplanes the moon was dissolving into blackness. The curtains moved with a life all their own.

Eight weeks. She had a big blue folder stuffed with lists of off-limits activities and substances. One page named herbs she had never heard of, black cohosh, blue cohosh, ma huang, thuja. There were known poisons, like wormwood. Had she ever been in the same room as wormwood? Had she ever been within a mile of these things?

Riley said the absinthe they drank in Amsterdam derived from wormwood. "You remember, the green liquor we drank on our honeymoon," he said, his grin indicating arousal. Sex was forbidden while she was bleeding, and these past weeks he was constantly grinning at her, hoping for good news. He pressed his thighs together. "It was on fire? The stuff that made us fuck like monkeys?"

"I thought that stuff was called booze," she said. "I thought it was called love. Or lust. And what do you mean, derived? I didn't ask for the etymology."

There were herbs on the list that surprised her, things she liked and would miss, aloe vera, ginger, parsley. "I feel like I can't even have parsley on the plate," she said, "or I might pick it up and chew on it. Just while I'm talking. You know how I am."

Riley knew how she was. He put his arm around her and offered her a drink of the lemonade from a tall glass promoting a science-fiction film with the image of a famous imaginary robot pointing a laser gun at her. "We'll have to tell all the waitresses," he said. "No parsley."

She said that wasn't enough. They were forgetful, daydreamy types. They would have to avoid diners for the next seven months.

It was a painful decision for people whose favorite meal was breakfast. "We'll never eat in a diner again, just yogurt at home," she said, starting to cry, wondering if the guilt was hormonal. "And we'll never have sex ever again. No more breakfast, no more sex."

She wanted Riley to say it was worth the wait, but he was tired of her indirect apologies and sighed to indicate this. It was the end of the second annual quarter, and he was beset by deadlines for the earnings projections it was his job to calculate. All day he sat rigidly in a cubicle, staring into a tiny laptop screen, using calculations and computer models to predict the future of the companies that paid him to pretend he knew the future so they could make decisions and then blame him if it went poorly. The last thing he wanted when he came home was a pouty wife, especially one who was imperceptibly expanding and bleeding on and off. Hazel gloomily pictured herself growing fatter in the coming months, eventually spilling out of her sweatsuit, hiding from the daylight. She thought a good wife would use this time to go down on her husband or something, but she feared that might be bad for the baby. Her nose pressed his arm, and her tears dampened his sleeve. He patted her shoulder and refused to complain. He was a good husband. His armpit smelled like roadkill, but she decided against mentioning it.

Nine weeks. Three more and the first trimester would end. This did not mean they would be out of the woods, said Dr. Kornblum. It meant they would be out of the first trimester, the statistically grim woods where eighty percent of miscarriages occurred. Dr. Kornblum said she was confident that at that point, the odds would favor them even more.

"Even more than they do now," she hastened to add. She smiled calmly. She was about the same age, early thirties, with long brown hair and with her first name, Natalie, sewn in cursive on the breast of her white coat. She spoke in the steady, measured tones of a surfer who long ago abandoned her board for a doctor's coat and a stethoscope but still remembered how to be cool. She was unflappable. "The heartbeat is steady. It could be stronger, but we see growth, which is promising. In a few weeks maybe things will be better. Why don't you come back in two or three weeks? Don't be afraid to call me at home."

Outside the clinic, women pushed strollers with heavy-duty rotating double wheels. These reminded Hazel of off-road vehicles. The stroller makers had thought of everything. In the strollers, the babies lay protected from sun and public by visors and layers of soft pastel-colored blankets. The mothers wore sunglasses and yoga pants, and Hazel wondered if they would acknowledge her existence and even smile at her, once her pregnancy showed. She speculated that the women might all be going to the same place.

"To do baby yoga," she explained, jealous because all forms of exercise increased her bleeding, and she sometimes thought she might have to sit very, very still for the next seven months. "They have that, you know."

"I'm hungry," said Riley.

It was breakfast time, but they felt safe eating in this part of town, where there were no diners, only expensive restaurants more likely to serve kale than parsley if they used garnishes at all. They went into a narrow café with a painting of a naked East Asian woman on the wall. Her breasts, areolas, and nipples were twin trios of concentric circles, and the woman peered over them, at anyone who happened to look, with neutral eyes, as if to dare the looker to question whether she was art. Their granite table was so narrow that Hazel was careful putting her elbows on it, which was the impolite but comfortable thing to do. The menu offered many kinds of hamburgers and salads served with various forms of protein chopped up on top.

Riley grimaced and sighed through his nostrils over this misfortune. He disliked hamburgers almost as much as he disliked salads. Yet time was limited. He had to get to work and start looking at his computer so that he could invent the future. He chose a sandwich with enough dressings to totally conceal the beef patty from his taste buds. When the food came, everything looked too small. "Why isn't this easier?" he said. "Growing up was supposed to be the hard part."

"I think the only easy part is college," Hazel said. "And maybe your twenties. You're not already tired of the baby, are you?"

"I'm tired of many things, but I've yet to meet a baby."

"Maybe I should stuff some gauze up there," Hazel said.

"I'm tired of the clinic. All those pictures on the wall. Babies in baths, babies superimposed on fake movie posters, and I have yet to meet one of them," he said. "How much do you want to bet that most of those kids don't even look like that anymore?"

"They do seem crazy about babies," Hazel conceded. "Some people just want to work with that stage of life, I guess. Just like you only deal with a certain type of grown-up."

"I deal with reality," Riley said. "Okay, pretend reality that gets taken seriously." He dropped his half-eaten hamburger on his plate and scowled down at it. "I bet many of those children are much older now."

Ten weeks. The living room had become a museum of congratulations cards. Who knew this many people still considered them friends? Not Hazel. There were handwritten notes here from people she'd last seen near the end of college. And some of the cards from Riley's historical cohort came from the wives of men he casually referred to as shitheads. She opened the cards and set them on the floor like dominoes and knocked them over in designs, hearts and arabesques and a four-point star. She built a house.

She photographed these things and posted the images online at a social networking website. Right away, unemployed acquaintances sent little notes informing her how creative and talented she was, and she began to think she was dealing with crazy people on the Internet. When they began to congratulate her on her pregnancy and ask her personal questions about her development, she deleted the pictures and closed her account. She sat in the living room feeling vaguely soiled. She feared she had been very close to turning into a crazy person on the Internet.

Riley came home, and she made him talk about names.

"How can we?" he said. "We don't even know the sex."

"How many contingencies does your software allow for when modeling industry futures?" she said. "There are only two possibilities here."

"I should never have told you what I do."

She began to name the names she liked, and Riley rejected them one after another. Samantha, Fred, Claire, Donald, Tabitha, Lawrence, Heidi, Benjamin, Wilma, George, Genevieve, Brad.

"How many vetoes do I get?" he said.

"Unlimited," she said. "You're an executive power. How do you like David?"

Riley liked being an executive power. "David's all right. Let's put it on the Maybe list."

"There's a Maybe list?"

"Shouldn't there be? Have you thought this through?"

Hazel had a confession to make. "I have a confession to make," she said. "I already have a name for him."

"Him?" Riley looked cross for a moment. "Did Kornblum call while I was at work?"

"No, I just have a feeling."

"Oh." Riley was happy again. He was confident that he knew all about her feelings. "What's your name for him?"

"Henrik," she said.

"That sounds to me like a Viking name."

"Yes," she said. "I think of him as a little seafarer, setting out from a distant country."

"You're very strange," Riley told her. "If I had known how strange you really are, I would have knocked you up much earlier."

"Henrik's the Viking," Hazel said, "which makes us the peasants watching for him on the sea."

Eleven weeks. Something was wrong. The ultrasound technician's jaw had clamped tight, and her eyes studied the screen intently. She mumbled something about looking at Hazel's ovaries, then turned the probe. Images shifted to dark on the screen beside Hazel. A large pale torpedo shape moved across the screen, and then another did. Riley's forehead bunched with frown lines. Did he know an ovary to see one?

Hazel was going to ask a question, but the technician moved quickly, printing the photo, telling them to return to the waiting area. "Dr. Kornblum will be with you momentarily," she said and went quickly through the curtain and out the door.

Hazel was afraid. "Usually they let you listen to the heartbeat."

"That woman," Riley said, "was a total bitch. The way she looked at us? Sheesh."

Hazel tried to believe this. She could see Riley trying, too. But there was so little evidence that the technician had been a bitch that they said nothing as they waited, first in the waiting area, and then in a consulting room, where Hazel sat on the patient's bed and Riley sat in the doctor's wheeled chair and they both studied a poster with an illustration of a baby gestating in its mother's womb. The baby was packed and contoured around the woman's organs, and its eyes were closed like the eyes of a sleeping koala. Hazel wished the time would stretch out into an eternity of waiting, but soon she heard Dr. Kornblum coming down the hall. The doctor knocked, came in smiling at them, and shook their hands. Riley surrendered her chair, and then the doctor opened a folder she had brought and, without consulting it, began to speak.

"As you recall, you've been having some bleeding, and we were worried about the heartbeat," she said, looking first at Hazel and then at Riley, intent and focused, as if she were selling them a car. "We wanted the heartbeat to be stronger. It should have been. But we waited, hoping for the best because sometimes some bleeding happens in the first trimester. It is not normal but neither is it uncommon. Today we can see that there has been no more development since your last visit. The technician could not find a heartbeat." Dr. Kornblum was looking squarely at Hazel, reaching out and then placing her hand firmly on Hazel's shoulder. The hand was surprisingly light, and Hazel reached up and covered it with her own, as if she were in a position to give comfort. Dr. Kornblum continued to study her, unmoved, and Hazel supposed that Kornblum had been a doctor for some time now and could not be talked out of what she was telling them. "I am so sorry that this happened to you. What happens next is that your body will have to expel the material. You've been bleeding, which tells us that your body has been trying to do something for a while."

"Okay," said Hazel. She was crying, but only slightly. She looked at Riley. He leaned rigidly against the counter, arms tight across his chest, his stare inward, as if he had become bored and begun to daydream. He lifted his fist to his mouth and sank his teeth into the skin beneath the knuckle of his index finger.

Dr. Kornblum pulled a tissue from the dispenser in the wall and handed it to her. "These things happen at random, usually as a result of a genetic abnormality. It is likely that this embryo carried some form of what we call mental retardation, something like Down Syndrome. Whatever is wrong prevents it from developing further." Her warm hand squeezed Hazel's shoulder. "It was probably retarded or something like that."

Suddenly the doctor was talking in a lighter, faster voice, saying something about options. Options? The word turned in Hazel's mind like an oddly shaped rock. Apparently there were decisions to be made. Dr. Kornblum could give her pills to take at home before she went to bed, in the hope she would wake up bleeding heavily. Or she could have a procedure, right here in the clinic, first thing tomorrow morning. Dr. Kornblum would perform it herself. She promised it wouldn't hurt a bit. "I'll give you some Valium to relax you," she said. "I have an instrument that will vacuum out the material."

Hazel's queasy pregnant feeling was worse than usual now, like she might vomit. Maybe this was what people meant when they talked of motion sickness, which had always seemed made-up to her, even though she knew those people couldn't all be lying. She considered what the doctor had said. She disliked pills, and the thought of coming all the way back in the morning felt like an invitation to climb a mountain tomorrow. Besides, she was no longer sure she liked Dr. Kornblum after what she'd said about Henrik being retarded.

"I want to go home," she said. "If it's going to happen, let it."

Riley thought she should have the procedure performed. He said so when they got back to the apartment and were standing in the midst of the cards from all the people they would now have to tell to forget about the baby, and from a percentage of whom they would then have to accept condolence cards. The procedure, Riley said, sounded not only harmless but quick, and she could be free of that thing by tomorrow morning. That thing. She wanted it gone, didn't she? His eyes were dark and tearful, and he was very angry suddenly, though not with her. He was angry with Henrik.

"The little fucker tricked us," he said with a grown man's unintentionally comic sadness. "It never meant to come out, just to waste our time and lie to us. I wish it was already gone." He sat down and got out his phone and began to send text messages to coworkers, telling them he would be working from home. By the time he had gotten out his laptop and turned it on, he had calmed down somewhat. His face looked drained and tired. It was 9:43 in the morning. He asked if he could cook her some breakfast.

She was starving. "Get takeout from Mack's," she said, referring to the diner up the street. She ignored his baleful eyes and wrapped a blanket around herself. She could not believe what he had said about Henrik, who may have been dead, but who was nonetheless part of them both. "Go on and order," she said. "You know what I like. But get some dessert, too. I could eat a horse."

Twelve weeks. Henrik was nearly half an inch long. Sinking in the water, falling into his red underwater cushion, he looked like an unbaked piece of pie dough. Hazel wondered whether she should call Riley. There was no point in it. He would close his laptop and come home, and then he would simply be here, too. It was better to let him work, finish a strong day's output, and return in the evening to news he would find a relief. She looked a last time into the swirled water. Henrik had been the last to turn against her. She closed the lid and pushed the lever.

The water washed Henrik down the pipe through several floors and a spider-infested basement, and then down a larger pipe, where he joined a river of sewage. The water was foul but swift, and he moved along unimpeded. Other rivers spilled in constantly, creating a communion of waters. He came to a whirlpool, plunged through a crack in the ceramic, and shot out into cleansing salt water. Without anchor he drifted gradually upward, among the dark shapes of aimless fish, passed a shark's dim eye, and whirled among pearly mullet until the surface lay just above, a blanket of shimmering sunlight. The ground beneath him fell away into blackness, and then there were no more fish, only the ceiling of light pressing down in steady ripples. Gradually the light vanished, and he was enclosed in a darkness that seemed never ending, until the light returned gradually. This process repeated itself many times. He came to a place where leafy green lianas hung from the surface, and the water was very still. Thick eels swam around him, their mouths smiling as they came together, coupling in spirals. One day the seaweeds and the eels were gone, and the water was colder, and the ceiling of light came and went as it had before. This happened so many times that Henrik lost count, even though he had nothing to do but count, because he had never learned numbers. He moved among tremendous masses of rough blue ice and found himself drifting in a frozen maze with giant skeletons trapped in its walls. His tiny black eyes, preserved by cold, watched the ceiling of light that had become constant. The light was brilliant and warm and had a carefree existence there on the frigid water that encouraged anyone who saw it to daydream. The dream of light stretched on and on, until it was collapsed into a single moment as Henrik was jolted from this state, snagged by a warm, faster current. One day, as harpoons plunged into the blue around him, he saw a great black whale break loose of their barbs, leaving ribbons of blood to drift toward the light as it dove hard into deeper blackness, never to return. He hovered over shipwrecks and coral reefs, saw the bones of broken ships, and one day he entered an ancient city where mermaids adored him. Some nights he settled gently on the headboard, just as Hazel dropped off to sleep.

SMILING DOWN AT ELLIE PARDO

✧

I.

After the Second World War an ambitious developer cleared woods east of the city, measured acre lots, and built colonial houses and cottages. Though he'd had a vision of white money flocking to the country, when the bank seized the land only half the houses had sold. In subsequent decades farmers razed most of the remaining forest to grow soybeans and corn, but when my parents bought the second house down from Woodacre Lane's dead end, enough timberland enclosed the neighborhood to pass off the setting as an enchanted forest. Throughout my boyhood I played ranger in this paradise, exploring each grove with my pellet gun in hand; I eliminated rabbits, possums, starlings, and blue jays, and made room for squirrels, cardinals, robins, migrating finches, and sparrows. My sense of what made a pest came from my taciturn parents, amateur gardeners who poisoned shrew burrows and smiled to see the furry rodents lying swollen among the vegetables and vines. When circumstance forced me back into the house of my childhood, which devastated my pride at the age of thirty-four, it was difficult to regard the little wood around the neighborhood without feeling a pinch of guilt. I'd buried so many varmints in mass graves behind the woodshed that the random stab of a spade could turn up a pile of white bones.

Yet I had not committed my crimes alone, and when I opened the paper to see Henry grinning suavely in an ad for his legal services, I knew our paths would cross in a city of eighty thousand factory hands and bankers. A divorce lawyer, he'd helped more than a hundred residents leave their spouses. He was like a movie star, only less popular. I lacked the patience to let small-town fate reunite us. I called him at the office, and soon we were passing weekends together.

2.

The night a neighbor let herself into Ellie Pardo's house and discovered Ellie cut to pieces in the basement, Henry and I were playing friends-turned-cops for money on Frogville's center table. Frogville was a neon-signed brick billiards house in the snowy fields south of the city. We'd come here a lot in high school, hoping to witness fights or solve the mysteries that surrounded getting laid. Teens still gathered in the stale heat with the same ambitions. They lined the vandalized walls, smoking clove cigarettes and Marlboros, watching the matches proceed on the twelve red-felted tables.

We were the oldest players in the bar, maybe the only ones of drinking age, though a lot of kids had bottles in hand. What made us stand out more was the muscular guy in the police uniform handing over more ten- and twenty-dollar bills after the end of each game. The only thing that seemed to prevent him from killing Henry was the woman beside him, who was also a cop, though in her off-duty loveliness it was hard to believe.

"Don't be so upset, babe, now listen to me." Watching us with her big eyes, Officer Candy covered her hand with her mouth and talked strategy to Officer Perzik. Friends since childhood, they had become cops, fallen in love, and decided to get married. Maybe it had to do with the way they each looked in uniform.

Perzik's radio crackled unexpectedly, startling shooters at the next table. He liked to have his presence known while he pretended not to notice. These little disturbances of other games were his only solace as he lost and lost.

"I should arrest you both." Blue dust rained from his hairy fist as he chalked his cue. He missed an easy six-in-the-corner and shouted, loud enough to silence the hall for a moment.

"Am I up again already?" Henry asked. A slim pretty boy with parted hair and a suit, he never questioned his influence over the room, keeping a step ahead of his skeptics. As Perzik muttered in frustration over a mistake, he stepped right in to line up his shot. Though we were on a team together, he was the one winning. From the way Candy glared, as if wishing he'd get it over with so she could go home with her fiancé, I got the feeling he took their money often.

Striped tie thrown over his shoulder, his head in a hedge of smoke, Henry took the measure of a combo shot that would sink the nine. "You two must be broke by now, so here's where it gets interesting. If I make this," he said, "Candy's got to give me a kiss."

Candy sipped her beer and thought it over. "And if not?"

"Then Perzik gives you a kiss," I suggested.

"If I miss," Henry said, pretending to think about it, "then I'll give Candy a kiss."

"Fucking crook," Perzik griped. Having copied Henry's test answers in school, he'd recently admitted, while drunk, that his decent grade-point average had helped his admission to the police academy. He hated the thought of owing Henry; now he crossed the room to make a kid of about thirteen put out his cigarette. He came back to the table with his radio to his ear, frowning as he listened over the chatter and colliding balls.

"There's more than one recipe for success," Henry was telling Candy. He'd stuck a cigarette in the corner of his mouth, like a little gangster or newspaper man. She smiled at me and shook her head, as if amazed by the flirt this former examinations worrywart had become. This was the guy who used to pee his sleeping bag whenever he stayed the night at my house. The first time he aimed my rifle and took out a crow, he insisted that we hold a funeral for it. But I knew him to be a fast learner. Less than a month after he dropped that first bird, he roamed ahead of me in the woodlot, leaving the animals where they fell until the timber stood perfectly still.

"He's come a long way," I said.

Candy nodded. "If I'd have known he'd be such a success, I might have gone with him to homecoming sophomore year."

"You can't distract me." Henry made his shot and exhaled a stream of smoke, but Candy missed it because she'd noticed, as I had, the change in Perzik's face. His eyes had a hollow look, his lips were pressed white.

He put down the radio and looked at me. "Nolan, what's your parents' address?"

"Twelve-twenty-six Woodacre," I said. "Why?"

"Do you know a woman who lives at twelve-thirty-two?"

"Is that Ellie's place?" Henry held his cue in two hands, bending it a little. He'd passed many days in my neighborhood and had a right to worry about my parents' neighbor. She had been a kind of trial crush for us both.

"Yeah, it's Ellie Pardo's house," I said. My dread must have shown in my face, because Candy came over and stood by my side. "What happened to her?"

Perzik looked at me, the twitch in his mouth reminding me of the crass, deadpan answers he used to give in class. His throat worked and he said, "Somebody tied her up and killed her."

3.

Ellie Pardo bought the gable and ell house next door to our cottage when I was still new enough that strangers dropped in to meet me. She bought the last house on the street, blocked on two sides by the woods. What some people might have thought creepy she considered peaceful. She'd left a drunk who never got over high school graduation. The gossip said he had knocked her around a lot, but the woman I knew was indomitable.

A feisty Italian who always had a tray of lasagna in the oven or a red sauce bubbling on the stove, she jogged back and forth on our street each day, exposing her beautiful legs even to the wicked cold of our winters on the lake. She said that red thighs were a sign of good circulation. Most of our neighbors were elderly, but she stopped to talk to them all, running in place the whole time. Since she didn't discriminate by age we became friends shortly after I began to talk.

I often cut through her yard to go to the woods. Her kitchen window looked back on her shady plot, and when I passed by I'd look up to her working at the counter or standing over the stove. If she looked up we would wave at one another. I wasn't allowed to shoot any birds or rabbits in her yard, but she didn't mind if I used her snow to make snow prisoners and then executed them with a pellet to the head. Once she came out and helped me pack snow into plastic crates, and together we built a sturdy fort, despite the neighborhood's lack of boys needed for a good war. Ellie enjoyed her indulgence of the child next door, and our afternoon passed in harmony. Then Henry began to come over.

Henry was a small and sickly boy. He was winded easily and didn't like to fight, and in the presence of mean children he kept his head low and his mouth shut. Yet around nice children and interesting adults, no one was more animated and jovial. When I taught him how to load, pump, and aim my pellet gun, he was afraid to pull the trigger. He said he didn't want the kick to bruise him. When I convinced him to try a shot with a pillow between the stock and his shoulder, he pierced the empty soda can I'd put on a fence post. He ran to retrieve the container, and when he picked it up, admiring the puckered hole the pellet had made and how it had scraped away the can's green paint, he fashioned a new appreciation of technology.

The first time Ellie saw Henry and me in her yard, she was moved by the sight of the small boy whose head had been wrapped in a homemade red scarf. His exact little nose reminded her of the men in her family. She ran outside in sweats and a race T-shirt and called out to me. She asked me to introduce my friend, then brought us inside and made us look at a photo album. Sure enough, Henry could have been a long-lost, much younger brother. Ellie believed in the sacredness of family and culture, and she persuaded us to agree with her by feeding us slices of homemade pizza and bowls of steaming wedding soup.

Once, we'd eaten too much to hunt successfully, and Henry and I conferred about our visit with Ellie and agreed that we each saw an opportunity to improve our days. It involved keeping our after-school kill a little more discreet. Instead of cutting through yards with our grocery bags of bloody animals, we'd pick a path through the woods and bury the bodies behind my shed. Then we would stage a snowball fight that crossed from my yard into Ellie's, knowing she'd invite us in for a hot meal. Some days we deliberately starved ourselves at school, sitting beside one another at lunch, two ascetics among the devouring hundreds, to intensify the flavor of Ellie's creamy, tomatoey dishes and the ecstasy we felt as we stuffed the gooey morsels into our mouths. Ellie would sit at the table, presiding as we cleared our plates. She encouraged us to take seconds, and we couldn't say no, not to this beautiful woman so dedicated to pleasing us. Henry was more slap-happy than I was. Once his belly had distended, he'd sit back and sigh in his high-pitched voice, his bulging eyes in love with the act of smiling.

4.

A feeling of strangeness settled over me as we made our way from the pool hall to the parking lot. There was discussion about the logistics of our inebriated travel, but I just sat in the passenger seat of Henry's car. It was good that I hadn't driven to Frogville because the news about Ellie had reduced me to staring.

Soon we were moving along the roads to Woodacre, Henry steering his giant car between Officer Perzik's cruiser and Officer Candy's jeep. He was drunk, and as we passed between the twilit fields, his wheels crossed the center line and the shoulder many times. He cursed as we drove, intent on getting there, but I couldn't comprehend what he was saying. My mind had backed up to a point outside my body, flying over the three automobiles moving in a tight formation over the frozen highway. I could see a shadowed barn standing at the edge of a field against a staple line of trees. Hundreds of starlings alighted in the frozen furrows, only to flutter up again and trade places. The changing sky took on a pearly quality, full of a hard sunlight slowly grinding us into dust. Henry glanced at me as he rambled, his mouth unhappy and jagged. Gradually it came to me he was upset because Perzik, in the cruiser in front of us, would not exceed the speed limit.

Henry slammed a fist on the dashboard and, shaking his hand, shouted, "Why doesn't he turn on his fucking lights?"

The suburb hadn't seen a murder in over a decade, and the far end of the street was crowded with police cars, an ambulance, and almost everyone who lived in a house on Woodacre. As we parked at the end of the cruiser jam-up, I quickly looked for my parents and, not seeing them, put the task of finding them aside for the moment. Henry ran ahead of Perzik and Candy, and I followed him. Together we pushed through a line of vehicles and people that seemed to indicate Ellie's house. The front yard was outlined with yellow tape stretching around the trees at the edge of Ellie's yard. The dark windows of the house reflected the winter scene and the dour faces of onlookers. A woman in a parka talked loudly and quickly about how frightened she was. No one spoke to her. Police paced anxiously in the yard, trying to look busy.

Henry refused to recognize the police boundary. He was outraged by the official measure dividing officials from citizens. When he lifted the yellow tape a young cop pushed him back, saying, "Please, sir, you don't want to do that."

"Fuck you, I'm welcome in this house," said Henry. "I'm going in there."

"I'm afraid you're not," said the cop.

When Henry stepped back and made a fist, it was obvious that he was going to throw a punch. There was an interval in which the cop seemed to think outside himself, happily enumerating charges he would bring against Henry. Then he sidestepped the swerving blow and chased Henry into a zinnia, where they struggled and gritted their teeth at one another and then fell into the snow. Four more cops came running, and I knew Henry was in trouble if no one would come to his aid, preferably someone with more local influence than I had.

The neighbors silently watched the police restrain the man who'd played in their yards years before. They must have known him from his ads in the paper, but no one protested when one cop slapped him. The young cop straddled Henry's chest and prepared to pummel him, but Perzik had gotten there, and he stepped in and pushed him off. Big enough to make the other cops hesitate, Perzik seized Henry from the ground and thrust him in my direction. Henry stumbled forward, confused, while Perzik held up a hand and told the younger cop to let it go. Then they began to argue, other cops started to shout at Perzik, and soon the crowd's interest concentrated on the squabbling throng of men in navy blue uniforms. Henry hurried over to Candy and me. His nose was bleeding and he was crying.

"Nolan, can you get him out of here?" Candy asked me. "They'll arrest him if he sticks around."

Once I'd taken Henry's car keys and gotten him to put on his seatbelt, I searched the crowd for my parents. They were at their house now, up on the front stoop, looking over the heads of the crowd at the policemen locked in debate on Ellie's lawn. They wore no coats despite the cold, only sweaters, and they were holding one another, their gray hair and their glasses poor masks for the grief in their faces. My father saw me in the street, waved, and said something that alerted my mother to where I stood in the Cadillac's open door, and then she waved, too. I pointed at the roof of the car, and sniffling Henry beneath it, in an attempt to explain that I had to leave.

My father gave me a thumbs-up and a nod, and it was clear that I didn't need to explain myself to him or my mother. They'd seen the scuffle between Henry and the cop. For the time being they'd ceased to be my parents, and I'd ceased to be their son. We were just three sad people in a sad crowd.

5.

I didn't notice Ellie Pardo's unhappiness until I was in my teens and was suddenly tall. My new perspective proved my neighbor to be a tiny woman, though her age, wisdom, and arresting good looks gave her more authority over me than ever. I was a shy teenager, and I blushed when she teased me about my growth spurt.

She would come over and sit with Henry and me in the garage, where we had removed our shirts and hefted the dumbbells from my father's old weight set. We'd set up mirrors and took our self-improvement seriously, choking down protein drinks between sets, and maybe Ellie sat with us for a little comic relief from her monotonous routine of work and exercise. We didn't mind the intrusion, and we held in our stomachs and kept our arms flexed just in case she wanted to check us out. We were average-looking boys without girlfriends. We didn't even have girl buddies to happen into romance with. Yet here was this beautiful woman whose deep green eyes seemed to see into us, talking about love.

"I'm through looking for men," she'd say with total certainty. "They can come to me from now on. You boys remember that. It's important for you to approach the woman. Men have forgotten that. Don't be shy. The girls will be glad to have you. And once you get one, don't stop telling her how much you like her."

She gave us tips to improve our lifting techniques. She told us when she noticed a new muscle line in an arm or an abdomen. I suspect she invented these lines on occasion, since her opinion of our physiques would drastically improve after a girl rejected one of us. I'd noticed how sometimes, when we'd cranked up the radio and were doing reps with our puny arms, that Ellie's attention would drift away from our workout studio. She'd explore a dark corner of the garage and look over one of the generic pastoral paintings my mother bought at garage sales. Henry and I would share a frown and keep flexing. Whatever she was missing, we couldn't identify it, and in those days the world of girls, music, and interesting subjects was expanding at such a rapid rate that, away from my garage and its weight bench, we easily forgot the melancholy silences of my next-door neighbor.

I wouldn't have an answer for years, until I came home from college, twenty-one years old, full of bravado and little else. I hadn't thought of Ellie in many months and was sitting with my father in the living room when we saw her Rollerblade past the window.

"I see Ellie's still keeping herself fit. Good for her," I said. At that age I spoke to adults as if I knew all about their pain. "But she never remarried. That's a real shame."

My patient father peered through his bifocals after her and said, "That woman has had her heart broken more times than anyone can count."

"She used to tell Henry and me that she'd given up on men."

My father chuckled. "They haven't given up on her. You think a woman like that can live in the suburbs, single, and not be asked on a date whenever she leaves the house?"

When I asked my mother why Ellie hadn't been over to say hello, she shrugged and looked over the boiling pots on the stove. She was canning frozen berries, and empty mason jars lined the countertop of her small kitchen. "She's going through one of her down periods. She'll be around when she's feeling better."

When I said that I remembered none of these "down periods," she gave me a long and skeptical look. "You really think you had any idea about what was going on in this neighborhood when you were a boy? Your father and I, we kept you good and ignorant. We wanted you to get out of this city."

When Ellie did stop over to say hello, she seemed anxious and distracted. She'd just finished running, but she smelled good when she came over and planted a kiss on my cheek. When I hugged her I was aware of her lithe back and the curve of her waist and that her perspiration had plastered single black hairs to her temples.

Her body grew rigid in my arms, and when we'd released each other I glimpsed a look of discomfort passing between my parents. When Ellie looked up at me again the friendly, open expression I had relied on as a child had been replaced by a look of courteous distance. I'd noticed this look in other women. She turned to my father and began to talk about the houses for sale on the street.

I didn't get to know Ellie as an adult, and when I visited my parents after that, she and I spoke less and less to one another. This last time I'd just seen her once, when she came home from grocery shopping while I scraped ice from my car's windshield. We'd limited the pleasantries to a wave. I was relieved when she didn't cross the snowy yard and ask about my misfortune. I glanced up as she was letting herself in through her front door, and in her self-conscious concentration on her keys, she seemed to soothe herself with the same thoughts.

Even so, she was my eternal next-door neighbor. Right up to the day when her body was found, I thought of Ellie Pardo whenever I saw an attractive older woman.

6.

Henry and I wound up in a sports bar with false wood walls that had framed hockey jerseys hanging on them. It was early and the place was deserted. The bartender, a young woman with a friendly round face, was playing a trivia game at the end of the bar.

Henry disappeared into the bathroom to clean up his face and straighten his suit. After fifteen minutes he still looked like he'd crawled out of a grave. His shirt was torn and a bruise grew under his right eye where the cop had hit him. He didn't say a word about the fight, and when we took seats at the bar, he asked the bartender to tune the television to a local channel. The story about Ellie's murder was broadcast on all the city's stations, and the grimness of jumping from channel to channel made us drink fast. Once the news stories began to echo each other,

I went to the pay telephone near the bathrooms and called my house.

My father answered, speaking in the quiet tones he used at the end of a long day. He asked, "Do you really want to know what happened?"

"Yes."

"You can't just go telling everyone this, you know."

"I know."

As he spoke I didn't hear another sound in the room, because I could see everything that had happened in Ellie's house, except I saw it happen in reverse, the order in which accounts of murders are told. Ellie had been dead for at least a day. An intruder had tied her up and held her prisoner in her basement rumpus room for perhaps twenty hours. There was speculation about what had gone on during that time which, once I'd heard it, I knew I would never repeat it, because I believed in Ellie's dignity. The police had named no suspects, and they theorized that the murderer was not someone from our community. They were watching the highways, shining lights in the forests, at that very moment.

When I returned to the bar, editing my father's story for Henry and the bartender, who by now shared our obsession, it occurred to me that over the past two days I'd stopped in my driveway and looked at Ellie's basement windows. In fact I had stopped each time as I passed them, to look at my reflection in the dark glass. I had done it out of nostalgia, remembering summer days I had used that glass as a mirror. I'd stand in front of those windows, flex my biceps, and imagine I saw growth. While she lay tortured or dead in her basement, I'd faced the window to where she lay, considering my teenaged narcissism. I concluded that Ellie must have laughed back then. Now it wasn't funny any way I looked at it.

The bartender poured all three of us shots. Henry questioned me relentlessly, as if he were examining me on the stand at the trial of his career. His intensity made the bartender uneasy, and after a while she left us to do something in the bright kitchen beyond a pair of swinging doors. When she'd gone, Henry questioned me even more aggressively. I swore to him that he knew as much as I did.

"Fuck, I want to know who did this," he said. "I'm not a violent man, Nolan, but if I get the chance I will kill this motherfucker."

I was surprised by the fervor of his feelings for my neighbor, but I also respected them. I remembered how she'd doted on him, spooning him red sauce from a pan, asking him for suggestions to improve the flavor. She never saw the boy who'd just ruthlessly killed as many as eleven birds and rabbits (we kept records), and tossed them one by one into a mass grave. Henry came from a nice-enough family, but when Ellie touched him on the head and said sweet things to him, his dreamy smile made it obvious that no one else treated him that well.

He revealed more after hours of drinking, after we'd staggered through the dark lot to his car. Inside we waited for the heater to work and watched our breath rise through the air. Henry switched on the dome light and turned to me. Even in the shadows I could see the drunken agony in his face. "I can't drive right now, but we got to go somewhere. I got something I got to tell you."

"What's that?"

"I loved her."

"Sure you did. I loved her, too."

"No. No. I loved her, loved her. I dated her. She used to stay at my house."

I stared at him, feeling betrayed, unwilling to believe. Ellie had been in her fifties. She had still been remarkably attractive, but she was only about ten years younger than my parents, whom middle age had molded into brittle likenesses of more vigorous people. Despite his small stature, despite her enduring fitness, Henry struck me as too hard-bodied and athletic for someone like Ellie.

"It wasn't a secret," he said. "She wanted to keep it quiet, but people knew. Everybody knew. I'm surprised you didn't. I guess you were gone."

"How long?" I asked. "When did this happen? How could you? She was like a guru to us. How can you sleep with a guru?"

"It went on for like ten months. Three years ago. It just happened. We saw each other at a church festival, and we knew. Things happen, man."

I didn't know what to tell him. I wanted him to take back what he'd said, to admit that he'd told a tasteless joke. I wanted things back the old way, where I had been between them. Instead we drove around the city and drank a case of beer. We had nothing to say to one another that we had not said in high school, so we drove to the shore and climbed the off-limits hill where kids broke their legs and wrists sledding each year. A sheet of gray ice covered the lake, and the stars flared in the mute black sky. Behind and around us, families slept in old farmhouses. We drank and pitched our cans at them, pretending we threw bombs that traveled far and destroyed.

"I don't have anything of hers. Just the stuff she gave me," Henry lamented. "I wished she'd left a single bra or something. Even a comb with some of her hair would be something."

At the time he told me this, my level of intoxication made me incapable of answering. But I understood, and to show this I nodded and then put my forehead on his shoulder.

I woke up later, realized I'd passed out, and saw us speeding toward a wall of plowed snow in a deserted parking lot. Beside me, Henry slurred a statement, then punched on the brake and spun his wheel. The car seemed to turn in slow motion. Dark sky rotated over icy lot. We came to a stop and rested. Henry lifted a hand and pointed. A police car was coming across the lot. He moved his mouth a few times before words came out. "We're fucked."

The car door opened, and Officer Candy got out. I was relieved but Henry didn't appear to care. She leaned in through his window and looked at the empties in the backseat. "What the hell are you guys doing?"

Henry let his head fall against the headrest. "We're looking for the killer."

Candy made us leave the car in the parking lot and drove us to Henry's in her cruiser. Once we'd helped Henry to his bed, I made a spot for myself on the couch with some blankets and a throw pillow. I was awake now, and Candy was in no rush to go back out into the cold. It was five in the morning, and she doubted anything would happen for a few hours. She said most of the troublemakers had passed out or decided to stay in by four. She'd only picked up the shift because she thought police would be out looking for Henry.

"He'll have to watch himself for a while," she said, rocking slightly on the edge of a blue recliner. "But this will pass over."

I enjoyed sitting in the heat with Candy, looking at the law titles in Henry's bookcases, and I began to regret that I did not grieve for my neighbor more than I did. There were too many years missing for me to say I knew her any longer. I asked Candy, "Are you worried?"

"About what?"

"That you're in here with us, and there's a killer out there?"

Candy looked at me the way a big sister might her naïve little brother. "No. Not unless he's the sort of killer who kills indiscriminately. There aren't many of those." She stretched her feet and formed a smile faintly manic from staying up for too long. She settled into the soft recesses of the chair and raised her girlish eyes to the ceiling.

"Did you know Ellie?"

She shook her head.

"Are you sad?"

She thought this over for a while, and then she said, "Disturbed. I'm disturbed." Then she looked at me and shrugged. "I'm a cop. It's my job to be disturbed."

7.

A few days later, the police had not arrested anyone. I watched every edition of the news and absorbed all of the details printed in the newspapers. I was sleeping poorly, wakened by creaks and winds. My heart beat rapidly, and I could read signs from great distances. Nervous energy set my fingers in constant motion, and my mind tuned easily to the demands of any task. I completed crossword puzzles and did chores my parents would never do themselves, like organizing the basement and garage. It snowed, and I shoveled driveways for ten bucks a job, which was less than I could have charged but which was an even trade for the effort it required. I needed something to do, people to speak with. Candy and Perzik had to work shifts, and Henry had no time between working with clients and privately grieving.

Beside ours, Ellie's house was a constant reminder of the gruesome crime. When I could stand it no longer, I slipped under the yellow tape and entered the house through the back door. It was cold inside. Someone had turned off the heat before the cops left, and I guessed that sometimes the mind turns to practical thought when nothing good can come of a situation. The kitchen was immaculate, but the dining room table lay overturned. I went downstairs and saw where they'd outlined her body on the carpet, over the massive brown stain, the part of her the police and medics could not remove. The shape in which she'd lain reminded me of the slumped body of a rabbit, and I was sorry that the woman had seen me walking around with a gun. I tried to imagine Ellie's final hours, the view of my parents' driveway and me intermittently, smiling down. It was possible that she'd decided to hope to be saved, and then optimistically put herself to sleep. I hoped she got that small mercy. I walked around the basement, looking into closets and corners. Of course the place was empty and my actions were unreasonable, but it made me feel a little better, knowing I was alone in there.

I heard someone upstairs, someone with my mother's heavy breathing. She called, "Nolan?" She stopped at the top of the steps and would go no further. "Come up out of there and come home."

When I reached her in the hallway, she was nervous that we would be caught inside Ellie's house and entangled in the police's business, but once we were outside she sighed and looked across the snowy yard to the gray, leafless trees. "I never thought I'd have to be afraid here," she said.

"Don't be," I said. "There's the police. There's Dad. There's me."

She took little comfort in these words and told me to go ahead and walk back in my original footprints. There was only one set, meaning she must have taken long strides for a woman her height. When I looked back, she was bent over, using her winter hat to fill in the impressions of my shoes.

8.

Eight days after they found Ellie, although the police knew nothing and it seemed as if we'd wait forever for the murderer's capture, the community held an Italian supper in the dead woman's honor.

They rented a hall in town and threw a party. My parents wouldn't have missed it for the world. Community parties were customary for their generation, which had grown up on city blocks and come of age at the right time to attend Woodstock.

My mother bought a new dress, and my father had a suit dry-cleaned. I was less dressed up than they, letting my button-down shirt hang over my belt, and felt surprised to see them so dressed up, though what amazed me was the collage they carried downstairs together. My mother had bought a piece of poster board and covered it with photographs from over the years. I charted Ellie's changing personal style over three decades, from plainly dressed city girl to middle-aged beauty in a cocktail dress.

"She's been working on this since it happened," my father said, a little proud.

"I think she'd have liked it," said my mother.

They were so excited over this touch of junior high sentimentality that I could do nothing but agree with them.

The reception was a hit. The Italian American Society provided checkered table cloths, a traditional Italian ensemble, and a delicious spaghetti dinner. The tickets sold out in advance, but when a crowd gathered outside the hall, the people at the door started taking donations. There weren't enough seats, so people stood around, twirling pasta on forks, munching on garlic bread, drinking cheap red wine. Music played, Ellie's friends gave speeches, people bawled and held each other.

I leaned against the bar with Henry, Perzik, and Candy. We drank beer and didn't say much. It was really a party for older people. I was happy with the turnout and the event and was glad to see my parents enjoying themselves. They stood holding their collage and told stories that accompanied the pictures.

Henry was getting drunk, complaining about the dinner. "These people didn't know her. What a lot of bull. They went on living their lives while she sat in that house by herself."

Perzik put his arm around Candy and stared down at Henry with stony disdain. "Cut it out. This is really nice. Look at that collage that Nolan's mother made. Show a little respect."

"Shut the fuck up, Perzik, you meatcart."

Candy took Henry's hand. "Hey, take it easy."

I gave Perzik a frown, entreating him to be patient since there was more than he knew to our friend's anguish. He whistled a brief note and walked away.

Henry ignored his departure. He glared at Candy, who playfully mocked his grimace. Henry wasn't laughing. He said, "We should be out picking the houses to pieces, looking for the guy. He could be in this room right now. I can't stand it."

"But this is a great thing, what the community's doing," said Candy. "You know?"

"I'm going," said Henry. He walked away from us toward the door and knocked his shoulder against an unwitting man in a fire department T-shirt. The fireman looked up, startled, and laughed at the receding smaller figure.

I sympathized with Henry. He'd loved Ellie Pardo, and it hadn't worked out, but I guessed he'd gone on hoping that it might. The things that surrounded me, the dinner, the music, the reminiscences, held nothing for him. I asked Candy to tell my parents that I had a ride home; then I hurried out after him.

9.

A few nights earlier I'd gotten out of bed, thirsty for cold water, and found my father standing at the sink in the dark kitchen, looking through the window at Ellie's house. I joined him, and he accepted my company without a word, stepping aside to give me room. In the moonlight the house looked like the closed face of a man buried to his neck. The yellow Caution tape shimmered in the wind. We could see the basement window, where for a certain amount of time we might have seen her in her distress, had we put our faces to the glass.

"Just watching for punk kids."

"There's nobody out there."

My father continued to frown at the house. He seemed frail in his pajamas; the key to his biology was winding down. When I suggested that he return to his bed, he would not budge. His fists trembled, but when I put my arm around his shoulders he turned away.

"She was so nice," he said bitterly. "She was so goddamn nice."

"I know."

"She was good to you."

"I know."

"All you had to do was be yourself, and she went on being an angel. I don't know what sort of person can't understand that." He looked up at me. "Nobody asked for this."

I couldn't tell him that sometimes you don't ask for what you have: a certain distance from the people, the right to be aloof. I knew this, and I also knew that philosophy is worthless just after a loss. So I told my father that he was right.

10.

Eventually the police would find their man, some younger creep Ellie worked with, a pimply faced goblin who had built a shrine to her in his basement and filled it with souvenirs from her house. The news would put to rest any remaining questions Henry or I had about what had happened that night. And by then I'd be gone, in another city entirely, training for a new cubicle, and it would prove a very easy thing to put off telephoning an old friend. When we did talk finally, we had little to say about Ellie or her killer or what happened the night of her memorial party, and the feeling between us was so poisoned that we hung up after ten or fifteen minutes of braying false good cheer.

After leaving the reception hall that night, we drove out toward the lake, like teenagers restless to skip town for a few hours. As we moved across the flat blue land, past little woods and silos and solitary houses, the conviviality of Ellie's dinner seemed more and more a figment of wishful memory. It seemed rather that the laughter and the music had been the sounds made by people who wanted to distract themselves from the dark silence we now encountered along the shore. Out here we could stop at any point and look out on the water, to see that the dark and the silence had no end. They were simply the shade and texture that remained when the day burned out.

Henry was a harsh man in the green light of the dashboard. "Those people are cowards," he said. "I guess a role to play's a good hiding spot."

"I guess."

It felt familiar and fitting, the pair of us in the front seat, moving along the road beside the perimeter of the state park, but when Henry said he saw a figure run along the tree line and plunge into the woods I began to doubt whether he was thinking clearly. He braked hard, and we stopped just over the road's frosty shoulder.

Concentrating on a point in the trees, he reached across my lap and got a handgun out of the glove compartment.

"What are you doing?" I asked.

"I saw him," he told me. "He's right back there. I saw the motherfucker."

All I saw were the woods at night. "Really?"

Ignoring any doubt in my tone, he removed the gun's magazine. He pointed it at the ceiling, and I eased up against the door as he counted the bullets inside.

The sunken ground he had indicated was covered with small ridges of snow collapsing on themselves. There were many holes, and it was impossible to see footprints. There was no telling what was out there. I looked at Henry, bent furiously at the window, studying the darkness, and it was then that I began to second-guess myself. What were the chances that this would happen to the woman I grew up next door to? What were the odds that my best friend and I would track down her killer when the cops could not? But then, what did I know at the end of the day? I'd lost a career, moved home when I should have been making adult strides. I hadn't even known, even dreamed my best friend from childhood might actually take the woman of our dreams to bed. And there were far greater mysteries. Maybe Henry had seen the killer. I turned and looked out my window, then up the dark road, to make sure there was no one standing there. A heat began to run through my body, and my mouth dried up.

"Henry. Are you sure you saw someone?"

He stopped what he was doing and said, "Look. You can come with me or you can stay here. You can believe whatever you want."

"Let's go."

He opened the door. A cold breeze washed over my face and tongue, giving me a taste of the lake, a stand of naked trees, a sky prizing a moon. I got out on the passenger side. He fiddled with the safety on his gun and crunched down through the snow toward the trees. I zipped up my coat and walked a few feet behind him. He drew strength from my presence, standing taller, lengthening his steps. We came to the line of the forest and looked in at the shapes of the trees that scurried deep to a point where we could see nothing else. We breathed patient clouds.

Henry looked at me and nodded, indicating I should lead the way.

I stepped into the woods, through ice and into freezing water and mud, my friend walking just behind me. The snow provided enough reflection for me to lead the way between thin trunks, and every few seconds a dark movement in my peripheral vision caused me to look one way or another. Suddenly I became aware of something else, something real and breathing on the other side of the trees ahead, something I could not quite see. I stopped and held up my hand. Henry came beside me, breathing through his mouth, and held out the gun in front of him. The figure was tall and wide, moving slowly, almost undulating, all colors flashing faintly in the blackness of its silhouette. I heard a snort; snow crunched. My eyes adjusted, and I saw the shape of the deer, at the same time Henry fired off three rounds.

He stood, panting. I heard myself swear softly.

"Didn't it hear us?" His voice cracked as he said it, like that of a kid who's destroyed something of value. He held the gun before him, balanced on two hands, waiting for someone to take it away. "Why didn't it run?"

"She's probably starving. Sometimes they forage all winter."

We came nearer and looked at the dying doe. She kicked her hooves against a tree. Her breaths wheezed in and out slowly. Hunger had deranged her, and in a fit of idiotic blindness we'd killed her. There was nothing we could do but go home and try to pretend it hadn't happened. We couldn't bury her, not in the frozen earth. We were no detectives. We were barely even hunters.

"What should we do, Nolan?" Henry said.

Seeing he didn't want to accept the inevitable, I took the gun from his hands and aimed it at the deer. It had been a long time since I held a gun, but I recognized all the sensations. For a second I could hear all three of us breathing.

We wouldn't officially say good-bye for another few weeks. Still, I'm pretty sure Henry understood what was happening, there in the woods. I stood beside him one more time, as I had done on countless afternoons of our damned childhoods, and pretended ownership just long enough to claim a life.

TRANSLATION

High above, propped-open windows let ghostly winter light into the station. Pigeons fluttered in and out, a constant disturbance of wings. He had seen five trains arrive and empty, fill with new passengers, and depart. He was trying to remember where he had seen the mosaic tiled into the wall across the tracks. It showed Lazarus emerging from his tomb, unwrapping the bluish shroud from his head as he walked out before the crowd. His arms were pale green by contrast to the peach-colored faces and arms of on-lookers, his posture upright and solemn, as if the experience of death and resurrection had turned the former beggar into something other than human.

He had seen this in a church somewhere. A long time back. He could remember neither the name of the church nor the city, though he knew, studying the scene, he was not religious. His memory was blank, a dark sea of implications throwing him back into the present moment. He had come down here after waking up in a dingy hotel room with only a train pass, forty-nine crumpled dollars and change, and a ring of keys in his possession. There were no cards, no phone. In the emergency room at the hospital he had waited more than an hour between two patients with more visible woes—a boy with a broken nose and a bloody shirt-front and a shivering woman with blue lips—before the nagging certainty that there was nothing wrong with him, at least not physically, won out, and he got up and walked out, feeling chills of liberation as he hurried away from the automated doors.

He reached into his pocket and took out the keys and ran a finger over their teeth. They were colored silver and dull gold. These details told him nothing.

A light appeared down the dark tunnel, and a rapid transit train screamed and clattered into the station, car after car of yellow-lit faces looking dully out. An internal clock, not a watch or other conventional timepiece, but a mechanism in him measuring time in its own way, prodded him to get up—perhaps motion would jog something loose, a street name, a trusted face. He looked into the dark window of the door and was momentarily stunned by the sight of himself: shock of black hair, face molded tightly to the skull beneath.

The car was full, the seats and the standing room at the front taken. He moved through making as little contact as he could, aware of faces pinching with annoyance as he eased by. In the back corner he came face-to-face with a small woman in a white and black plaid wool coat. Her blue eyes looked surprised to see him. She did not look away as he took hold of the pole beside her and the train resumed moving.

Passengers swayed as the car rocked back and forth along the rail. He felt her watching and wondered, if he knew her, how to explain himself. She sighed lightly, with what sounded like real disappointment. He turned back and gave a smile which might be an apology or just polite.

She frowned. "One of your moods today?"

"Sorry?"

"One of your moods."

"I guess. I don't know."

She had a wide pale face that was used to smiling. "Is something wrong? Are you feeling sick?"

"Both, you could say." He looked around at the nearby passengers. Only an old woman, looking tired to the point of anger, paid them any attention. "See," he said, leaning in close, "I'm having trouble remembering."

This won him a bigger smile. He supposed he must be a playful enough person to be considered a character.

"What do you mean?" she said, wrinkling her nose.

"I mean I think I've got amnesia. Like what people get in the movies."

"Stop."

"Really. I woke up in this hotel room this morning without a wallet. It looked like I'd been there awhile."

"What hotel?"

"One near the station. The Arms."

"You stayed there?"

"I guess. I woke up there." He paused, wondering if he should say more. She held to the overhead bar with white wool mittens and looked him over. He wanted to talk to someone, put what he knew into words, to see if he'd missed something. "I kind of panicked and left. I felt like I knew the last station, the one with Lazarus on the wall."

"Grant and Riverside," she said. "Okay."

"Maybe I live near there."

She smiled more widely. "Are you serious?"

He swallowed roughly, his face still hot, and nodded.

She took a step closer and lowered her voice. "Oh my God, Marcus. What are you going to do?"

"So it's Marcus." The sound did not fit him like a name. But she said it with conviction, and she had recognized him, after all. "I'm not sure. Should I go to the hospital? The police?"

"You don't look like you were mugged." She reached out to touch his hair. He let her. It was pleasant and delicate, and she was comfortable putting her hands on him. The sensation felt vaguely familiar.

"I don't feel like I was hurt in any way. In fact, I feel rested." He flipped up the lapels of his pea coat and bounced his shoulders like a greaser in a leather jacket. "I feel spry."

"Something's wrong with you," she said. "Listen, we're almost to my stop. Come with me."

"It's been a few weeks since I heard from you." She tore open a brown packet and poured sugar pellets into her coffee. She began to stir with her spoon, rattling the sides of the mug, then slowing so the light toffee-colored froth swirled on the darker liquid. She went on quietly. "You used to get on the train each morning at the same time. Always at the same spot on the platform. You stood next to me riding to work for six months. We would look at each other, but you never would talk to me. I thought it was because you were married. I thought it was for the best. I was mixed up with a married man one time, and it turned out bad."

He looked at his left hand and its naked ring finger. He wondered if he had lost it, sold it, left it someplace.

"Your wife left," she said, under her breath, as if she both feared and hoped the words would sting.

"Shortest marriage in history. Most painless, too." He did not feel like laughing. They were in a coffeehouse in the lobby of a building near her job, crowded into a tiny circular table beside the cold window. Around them strangers sat typing at laptops, reading newspapers, eating, talking, stealing looks at each other. Outside a bum in a soiled-looking green coat held out a cardboard sign for bundled-up pedestrians to read. He was sure he usually avoided places like this. "I feel exposed here," he said quietly. "Like there's no privacy. Like that's kind of the idea of these places."

"That's what you always say," she said. "I can never get you to come here with me."

He saw, among other things, she did not fully believe him. This news must be difficult to hear from someone you know, he reflected, especially if, as she said, it had been weeks. "Does that mean you and I were together? Is that why my wife left?"

She rested her chin on her hand, looking toward the brightly lighted glass counter filled with Danishes and bagels. "No. Not yet. We were being careful. Your wife left for some other reason. You never said. You didn't like to talk about it." She turned to him, narrowing her eyes with something new: the fatigue that sets in after sadness runs out. "You were always a mess."

His face burned with embarrassment. He saw how he must look, either like someone mentally ill or like a total creep, depending on whether or not she believed him. "Look, I'm sorry."

"No, it's fine," she said, with a swift, learned politeness.

"I guess I should go, try to figure out more stuff."

"I have to get to the office."

"Where do I work?" he said. "I have a job, right?" He was aware a girl at the next table had stopped reading her novel to eavesdrop. "I feel like the kind of person who would have a job."

She had stopped buttoning her coat halfway. Her face was soft with pity. She reached across the table and he could see she thought he was out of his mind—it occurred to him he was, in a manner of speaking. She petted his hand as if it were a wounded bird. "You need to see someone, Marcus."

He half stood, and his chair scraped noisily across the tiles. He had disrupted the moderate coffee bar noisiness, and customers were staring. "Seriously. Can you tell me?"

"You worked at Saint Anthony's College. You taught classical literature and theater there. But you lost your job. Don't ask me why. You never gave me a straight answer." She turned and headed for the door, holding her pastel blue purse so low it hovered over the dirty pools on the orange tiles.

He went out after her into the bitterly cold morning. Buildings of stone and steel and glass loomed up massively, their upper stories lost in vapors, echoing the slishing, honking cars. A bank of granite-colored clouds threatened more snow, and out across the drifts and avenues flurries danced. The air was blue and gray. He walked beside her, neither of them speaking, to the corner, separation imminent.

"Don't ask me to introduce myself to you again," she said sharply.

"I won't. Look, I'm not making this up. You shouldn't be offended." He sensed the words contradicted something that had passed between them. His face was getting cold, his ears stinging, his nose hairs stiffening into little birds' nests. Winds came up constantly now, and the right side of his coat flapped open.

She lifted her purse and hung it on her shoulder. "You used to tell me about what your mother was like right before she died," she said. "How terrible it was that she never knew you anymore. You talked about how hard it was that you didn't have any other relatives, how you were standing with her knowing she didn't remember the only person she had left. It sounded so lonely."

"She had Alzheimer's," he ventured.

She nodded. "It got really advanced, until she was just an old lady with the mind of a girl. That's what you said."

"Do you think that's what's happening to me?" he said.

"I think you're too young. But I don't know." She sighed. "I don't know, Marcus. I don't know." She took a tortoiseshell card wallet from her purse and gave him a rose-colored business card. *Laura.* "Call me when you find something out. Or if you need something."

"Great color," he said.

She nodded her head quickly. "I know."

As he approached the red brick classics building, two youngish women on the front stoop stubbed out cigarettes in the cement ashtray and disappeared through the heavy cream-painted wooden doors. He had seen their faces when they saw him coming and was sure they were avoiding him. He walked up the salted steps and, standing before the great brass doorknobs, took a last look at the small snowbound campus, a haven in the middle of the city. Pines and naked beeches and maples grew tall over Georgian-style buildings and sidewalks dark with melted snow. It looked like an ideal place to teach, quiet and rich, a shelter for student theatrics.

Save for a few sparsely attended classes, the building seemed empty. A white-bearded man speaking in Hebrew to a class of five students looked up from his desk, saw him, and paused to stare for a moment, then resumed his lecture.

He found the main office on the second floor. The student secretary, a short girl with pink hair and blue- and green-winged angels tattooed on her chunky arms, looked up from the computer where she was reading messages on a web page featuring a picture of her dancing at a concert. She smiled kindly at him. "Hey, Dr. Schwartz. I didn't know you were still around."

He looked around the suite at the closed doors with dark windows. The white names stenciled on their black placards were uncannily familiar. "Not many people around."

"Friday." She shrugged and glanced at her computer screen, smiled at something there, looked back at him. "Are you still moving out of your office?"

He nodded and started toward the hallway beyond her, when

she rolled her chair back and pointed in the other direction, toward a narrow half-lighted room behind him. The wall was a hive of rectangular wooden mail slots.

"Your box is full. Let me know when you've decided on an address for forwarding, and I'll take care of that for you."

"Thanks." He slipped into the narrow space, scanning the last names, one beneath each mailbox. It was a confusing system, alphabetized horizontally, and several of the slots were full enough to meet the secretary's description. He glanced over and saw her frowning as she watched. "Um," he said.

"Down two," she instructed.

"Aha." The opening was stuffed with letters and two bulging envelopes he guessed contained journals or books. He pulled them out in a thick stack and hurried past the girl into the tight corridor of faculty offices. He read the name signs on the doors as he went, looking for the one assigned him—Marcus Schwartz. He stepped over cardboard boxes full of dropped-off and graded student papers, glanced at articles and cartoons taped up as semipublic statements. Passing an open doorway he saw he had interrupted two presumable faculty members: a man wearing a T-shirt and jeans, his salt and pepper hair held up with hair glue, sprawled out in a chair before the desk of a woman with striking hazel eyes and curly gray hair to her shoulders. They had been talking in low voices, and when he passed they turned to look, the man with raised eyebrows and the woman with an astonished smile.

"Hi, Marcus," she called.

"Hey," muttered the man, turning his head to look elsewhere.

He lifted a hand in greeting and hurried on, terrified by the prospect of academic banter, with its mazes of connotations and pauses, and nearly missed the name he was looking for. He got out the keys, intending to lock himself in, and tried four before one fit the knob.

If he was this person, Marcus Schwartz, he had kept a messy office by his own standards, though he immediately liked the large map of the ancient world taped to the wall: its land was condensed into a honey-colored croissant resting on a swirled blue plate called *Ocean*. Books lay scattered across the desk, overturned or propped open with coffee mugs and other books. A brick of student papers slumped on the front left corner; bookshelves bulged. Aside from the map and wrappers and empty to-go coffee cups, there were no personal effects. He sat in his chair and switched on his computer screen. The desktop and e-mail account had been left open. Letters and memos lay around like fallen leaves.

He opened the paper mail, most of it garbage, memos and ads and newsletters, and found a letter addressing Dr. Schwartz. It was from a publishing house called Triton, and it told of a decision to pulp the remaining copies of a book of Ovid's *Metamorphoses* Marcus Schwartz had translated.

Strange, he knew Latin, he found, old and new, as various quotations floated to the surface of his mind. He knew several languages. He ran his eyes over the titles on the shelf, their words blurring together. Even if the translation did not tell him who he was—or what had happened to him, if he was Marcus Schwartz—he felt sure it contained a clue. The publisher's letter said no more than, *Given the overwhelming evidence of willful falsification in this matter, Triton Press sees no alternative but to proceed with the recall and destruction of this edition, and with the severance of all ties to its author.* He read through the e-mails. Most were student questions about grades. He deleted them, presuming they were the department's concern now. He read the more personal correspondence, condolences from Schwartz's former students, colleagues, and friends. Many mentioned the insignificance—one, the mischief—of Schwartz's act, but none said what he had done.

There was an article on the Saint Anthony student paper website titled *Professor Resigns after Accusations of Academic Dishonesty*. It said Marcus Schwartz, a translator who taught classics and theater, had quit after being accused of adding an apocryphal story to Ovid's *Metamorphoses*, claiming to have discovered a new fragment. The article described how other scholars concluded no such fragment existed, speculating Schwartz himself wrote the tale. The counterfeit myth was not described.

He searched the office, taking the books one at a time from the shelf and then tossing them aside onto the floor. Soon he had made such a pile that he was put in mind of a bonfire ready for ignition, and he had moved on to ferreting out books concealed under papers when someone knocked at the door. He ignored the disturbance and gave the room a final scan. Odd he would not have a copy of his own book in his university office, where it seemed several should be lying around.

The knocking came again. "It's Catherine."

Deciding her voice sounded more eager to talk than to listen, he opened the door and looked down at the woman whose conversation he had interrupted earlier. She smoothed down the front of her maroon sweater over the waist of her gray skirt.

"Hey, Catherine," he said. "What's up?"

She looked down the corridor as if to ensure they were alone. "I didn't know if you would be back. Ever."

"Look at this mess. Can't just leave this behind."

"In all honesty," she said, looking past him, "I thought you would just abandon it. Just leave it all. I guess I do that, imagine people are more impetuous than I am, to live vicariously. How long has it been?"

"A while, I guess. I haven't really kept track. In fact, I'm actually about to step out, and I can't say when I'll be back."

"Listen, Marcus." She crossed her arms firmly across her chest and looked up into his eyes. "I just want you to know that some of us are behind you. No matter what the dean says. I've talked to friends at other schools, and I don't think this thing will dog you. You'll be okay."

His eyes moved past her earnestly trembling face to the office almost right across the hall. Through the open door he could see, beyond a desk covered in Faberge eggs and figurines, her shelves of hardcover books in shining dust jackets. "Thanks, Catherine, it means a lot. By the way, would you happen to have a copy of *Metamorphoses?*"

She tensed at the shoulders like a cornered animal. "Which one?"

"Mine."

"Oh." She pressed her lips together and breathed through her nose. "I'm sorry, Marcus. I sent mine back to Triton. I didn't want to, but mine was a gift edition, and Henry contacted me personally. They're so embarrassed, you know. And the bookstore here had already sent theirs back." She glanced away. "I didn't want to send it back. You know what it's like in this field. There are only so many places to publish."

Laura picked up on the third ring. "Hey," she said in a depthless monotone. He gathered that her cell phone informed her that the office of Marcus Schwartz was calling. Machines recognized Marcus Schwartz, he reflected, and would continue doing so until someone else took over that information. "I'm at lunch. Can I call you back?"

"I just have a quick question. It shouldn't compromise you at all."

"Sounds promising."

"Do you know my address? My home address, I mean."

She paused, breathing into the phone as she fiddled with something. "Yeah, hold on, it's in my purse. Are you ready?"

He wrote it down on a sticky yellow note and put it in his pocket. "Are you busy later?"

"I can't talk right now. Call me later."

Back on the train, seated beside the doors, he read vandalized ads for night schools and free background checks and glanced at the faces of fellow passengers, all of them looking forward to being elsewhere. The car was warm, and the linoleum was covered with puddles of melted ice. Outside the smeared plastic window a moderate snow was falling on the city and the snow-covered river. At each stop, a new mob of strangers boarded blowing clouds of breath, rubbing their hands together as they sought out open seats. An old woman wearing a pink parka and a plastic babushka sat in the space beside him, using her sharp little elbow to prod him into the corner. In place, she looked straight ahead, her wrinkled nose and frowning mouth framed tightly by her steel-colored hair and her shawl.

The train rushed forward over an elevated track, descended along a three-block stretch, and plunged into a tunnel under the city. As the daylight disappeared and the dark walls and vacant passageways came on, now visible, now gone, he felt the first clutches of fear in his chest. He was suddenly certain that he would not like what he was going to find in the apartment, that whatever lay hidden there would tie him forever to an awful crime. Who was Marcus Schwartz, anyway? Who had he been that he had forgotten who he was? The truth must be terrible, he thought, if he had somehow hidden it from himself. That the people who recognized him and the messages he'd read suggested he was a nice person pointed to secrecy, which frightened him more.

He stepped out in a crush of people onto the platform beside the ghoulish mosaic of Lazarus. The hustle of others moved him along quickly, down the long, bright white, domed tunnel, then up another flight to the bustling city street. Winter air descended onto his head and shoulders like a heavy blanket, stuffed his lungs with chill. He walked through black and gray slush past people hidden under long coats, scarves, hats. Many women were wearing fur-lined boots. He walked through the clouds of strangers' breath, past bright storefronts displaying gaudy jewelry and winter hats on mannequins dressed in form-fitting clothes. He watched out for the slush holes appearing suddenly underfoot. The blocks were long, but eventually he came to the address Laura had given him on a quiet street.

It was an eight-story brick building, old and faded and ugly, with a black fire escape zigzagging up the side. The doorman, seeing him wander onto the green doormat and stamp the ice from his loafers and soaked pant cuffs, came and let him in. He was an older man, with heavy jowls and thick folds in the cheeks around his smile. He nodded slowly in the manner of monolingual immigrants and ushered him toward the steel elevator doors.

He rode to the eighth floor and went to the apartment number Laura had given him. The hallway was dark, the walls covered in burgundy wallpaper, the red and orange carpet short and coarse. He looked through the peephole and saw dim daylight on the other side, the gray wateriness of depression. He knocked and waited, listened to the wood and heard nothing within. He took out his key ring and tried keys. His hands were shaking a little. The dead bolt turned on his second try.

Mail had piled up in a heap inside the door, and he smeared it across the foyer pushing his way in. The warm air held the wild stink of unwashed dishes and the life forms they favored, cigarettes and booze, garbage long ready to go out. The kitchen was as the stench portended—dirty dishes and pans and empty bottles appeared to have erupted from the sink and flowed out over the countertops. By the blankets and crushed pillow on the living room couch, he guessed Marcus Schwartz had been sleeping there, perhaps too drained to drag himself to bed when there was a television to keep him company. In the bedroom, the mattress was stripped bare and covered with wrinkled and dirty clothes. In the half-open drawers he found a pair of clean socks, briefs, dry jeans, a few shirts. Fresh jogging shoes on the closet floor. In the dingy bathroom, he looked at his weary reflection as he scrubbed his hands with hot water to warm them up and decided, as it appeared no one had been here for a while or would be soon, that he could take a shower. Afterward, shaved and washed, wearing Marcus Schwartz's clothes—which fit him well—he felt like someone else. He opened the medicine cabinet and found an old blue toothbrush and a curled tube of toothpaste.

In a spare bedroom that had been used as an office, he dug through bookshelves and the stacks of books left on the desk and in the corners. He could not find the translation by Marcus Schwartz. Only when he had given up searching did he notice the answering machine on the shelf above the writing desk, message button blinking red. He stood licking his lips, unsure about the situation. He felt now as if he were being guided toward some fate of Marcus Schwartz's design; after all, who else was responsible for all that had happened to him so far?

To know or not was not much of a choice. He pressed the button. An automated male voice informed him he had fifteen messages. The first was over thirteen days old. A woman's voice, husky and full of sadness, filled the room. He knew immediately he had heard it many times.

"It's Liz. I'm wondering if you're going to ever call. I know you're probably sitting there, all messed up and angry at me, but I wish you'd just pick up. Don't be such a baby. Pick up. I'm worried about you, okay?"

Seven of the messages were from Liz. Starting almost two weeks ago she had called once a day for six days, finally threatening to come over and use her key. In the seventh message, left on the evening of the seventh day, she reported stopping over and coming in, finding the place filthy as his place in Boston, which he guessed dated from college or grad school. He had not been there, she said; he should call her when he was sober and ready to talk. The rest of the messages were robocalls from politicians, credit card companies, insurance scams.

He picked up the phone, found Liz's number in the caller ID, and called her. It rang five times before she answered. She sounded in good spirits but a little detached, as if she were in the middle of vacuuming the house.

"It's me," he said.

"I see," she said. "So."

"I'm at the apartment now."

"Finally decided to call me back, I see."

"Yeah, sorry about that. I—"

"Don't apologize, Marcus. Don't do it." He saw her: a tall woman with a pretty, expressive face and long cinnamon-colored hair, pinching the bridge of her prominent nose, closing her eyes. "I'm really just not up for that right now. I kind of doubt you are, either."

"Something's happened."

"I don't want to hear about it. Really."

"I don't understand it."

"Marcus. You can do what you want to do to yourself. It's not my business any more. Listen, I screwed up, too, I'm just as much to blame as you are. We fucked it up a long time ago. I can't go into it. The thing with Jeff, and you, you were in a completely different world. And that shit with your job."

"Yeah," he said. "I guess maybe that's it."

"You guess? Jesus, Marcus, we were like a fucking case study. We started too young, forced it too long. Period." Her voice was filled with nostalgia and relief. She gave a long sniff. Then she spoke away from the mouthpiece. "Hold on a sec, okay? It's Marcus. Are you there? God, I wish you had called some other time. Jeff and I have got this thing at the Breton tonight. It's a little one-act we wrote together. We're just getting ready. Can I call you back?"

"Sure. But Liz, hold on."

"Yeah. What is it?"

"Do you have a copy of that book?"

It was where she said she'd leave it, in a manila envelope leaning at the foot of the townhouse door. She had left the lamp on, as she said she would, so he could see it there. A brass ashtray on a tall tripod stood beside the door, and he knew before he looked in it that he would see half-smoked menthols, their white butts stained with pink lipstick. He leaned and picked up the envelope. The name *Marcus* had been scrawled hastily across the paper in her large looping script, was sealed with a red sticker shaped like a heart. She used these for everyone, to represent her friendship, but he could imagine the pain she must have felt sealing this parcel. He tore open the package and removed the book, a black paperback with an image of a green ouroboros on the cover, beneath the title. He looked at the dark bay window beside the door, its white curtain concealing a living room, dining room, or some other room that called to mind a stage set. He wondered what it looked like, how the air inside smelled and felt. He felt compelled to ask for a glimpse, a taste, to join it temporarily, to knock on the heavy wood, to speak his name and be admitted. He knew they had plans tonight, that the house stood empty. He had heard the excitement in her voice.

He sat on the top stair and read through the table of contents. He knew these stories, had committed many to memory. He had been translating them almost twenty years, since his first days as an undergraduate, and still he loved their distance, their romance. He found what he was looking for right away. He read it twice and sat in the cold night, lost in vague thoughts, until he heard someone coming. It was a younger couple, still in their work clothes, stumbling drunkenly up the sidewalk. He imagined they had just come from happy hour somewhere, surrounded by strangers whose minute differences from them and each other made the world feel safe and rich. They passed through a streetlight. The man was tall, grinning under his thick-framed glasses. She was laughing hard with her eyes shut tight, her arm wrapped around his narrow waist. She had reached a state where all he said made her laugh harder, bent over by stomach cramps.

He watched them walk down the darkened street until they passed beyond his sight. Then he stood and walked, moving his stiffening joints through the cold air until they warmed and found a rhythm. He stopped at the corner and dropped the book into a black steel garbage can. The book hit the bottom and made a single dull echo. Seeing the yellow glow of a drugstore across the street, he proceeded to the pay telephone next to the door, took the scratched black receiver from the cradle, wiping it on his coat before he placed it beneath his ear. He dug out Laura's card and, in the yellow glare of the sign, read the neat printing on the soft rose-colored paper. He slid two quarters through the coin slot, looking through the glass. The shopkeeper leaned on the counter, reading a magazine over a display of lottery tickets.

"It's Marcus," he said when she answered, her voice tired and rough and curious.

"Where are you? Where is this number?"

"Some phone," he said. "I'm north of the city. Not far."

"I'm still at work," she said. "Another twenty minutes. Today has been a real bitch."

"Will it be too late to grab a bite somewhere?"

A long silence on her end, the hesitation that was a willingness to be convinced. "I don't know," she said. "What did you have in mind?"

"Not sure. I'm starving. Let's talk about it. I'll meet you at the station near there."

MNEMOSYNE AND THE PLAYWRIGHT

In Paphos there was a playwright who had been married off young and was terribly unhappy. His wife too was discontent. When she took a lover, the playwright, seeing no blame in either of them, prayed to Mnemosyne to make him forget himself and be thus freed from his misery. Because he had so faithfully mimicked human strife on the stage, Mnemosyne heard his prayer and appealed to Zeus, but the cloudsplitter remonstrated that it would not be sufficient for the playwright to forget himself while the memories of so many others held him in place. So the mother of the muses convinced the dream god Morpheus to kidnap the playwright and replace him with a double.

Many years passed and the playwright's family and friends had died or gone away. His double lived on, old and wild haired, wandering the street, harassing strangers and conversing with phantoms. The period when others found his antics amusing had long passed. The double was thought to be truly mad, and his wife now lived in the household of another man. It was only when he slept that the playwright woke in his replacement's dreams, never remembering what had come before.

Once more Mnemosyne went to Zeus and pleaded the playwright's case. The father of the gods looked down on the double, cavorting in the street in filthy rags, and took pity on the playwright. He decreed that not only should the playwright be restored to his rightful place, but that his youth would be returned to him, as a reward for his faithful sacrifice.

When the people saw that the soiled beggar had been transformed into a young man in full possession of his wits, they took a goat to the temple and slaughtered it in honor of the gods.

This is why in the city Paphos, when they see an old person dancing, they say, "It is unhappy memory, not time, that makes one grow old."

A DIFFICULT AGE

Look at it this way. Fourteen years old and I stand six feet two inches high, a lummox with charm like the muttering lord of the dead. Last summer most of my mom's breasts were removed, which is no excuse, though it is a reason I began to hate everyone. She shed her hair; I grew mine to my shoulders and dyed it black. Once partners in sarcasm, observers of amphibians in our Black Swamp surroundings, the parent-child duo that chatted past the zero hour, we have become strangers, willing to hurt with words. To ease life I roam the downstairs, now that she's as bald as Lionel, the boy on our front porch, listening after the doorbell's echo, his pipe-thin arms short and flared.

Lionel's baldness is self-imposed, and to ensure that no one mistakes this, he wears a heavy chain-link necklace and a black Megadeth T-shirt that portrays an emaciated man sweating bullets out of his forehead and chest onto a wooden table. Lionel is my age, has hounded blue eyes and crooked teeth, and lives in a slab house on the south side of this large park of Black Swamp forest, in a neighborhood of slab houses, a neighborhood with snarling dogs and no government, alongside the railroad tracks. He is my best friend, and for a long time was my only friend, until Brooke became pregnant, around the time the surgeons cut the tumors out of my mom. Until Brooke began driving him over in her old blue Stingray, the rumbling and rusted wonder of our minds, Lionel was forced to ride the dirt trails on his second-hand mountain bike to reach my house through the riparian forest.

I open the door. He waits, immune to the October cold, on the flagstones. Up high the clouds lie back over the stick trees. Brooke waits in the running car, her little eyes crinkled as she smokes a Kool.

"Don't ask," says Lionel. "Don't even bring it up. She got really really pissed off about five minutes ago, and before she got pissed off she was already crazy. All right there, big guy?" He claps my shoulder, laughs nervously. Being so much smaller, he enjoys the idea of pushing me around. I hardly notice this. He slips past me and opens the front door. "Hi, Mrs. Wheeler, bye, Mrs. Wheeler!"

My mom's up in her room, watching the TV shows we once watched, in the days she had breasts and long messy hair and did more than eat frozen dinners in bed. Skeletal, loose-skinned, and bald like an old man, she sits under blankets and pink wool cap next to the much-hated wig of bouncy brown-blonde hair on the nightstand, the lesser world of *Cheers* going on inside the television, her gun in a drawer and her ranger's uniform hanging in the closet, the park service radio burbling on the dresser. At the sound of Lionel's shout she savors a blend of fondness and anger. She won't call back, though she smirks, and not because teasing Sam has once again irked Diane into a sexy shouting match. She is getting slowly better, putting all of her power pills into a pile. Her strength is returning, having once left her stoned and waxy in a hospital bed — that night I sat in the waiting area I half-expected to see her ghost wander past the nurse's station, as if in search of a restroom. Instead we came back here, where she glides through the kitchen in a pink gown. She sniffs the rot in the room and tells me to sweep the sparrows out of the fireplace, to repair the screen at the top of the chimney. She watches, silent, vigilant only until the job is finished, then departs without a word. The commercial break echoes from her bedroom, and the quiet fills with her steady breathing until her door shuts.

When I think of her coming out of there, I shiver a little.

In the sound of ticking clock-and-quiet house and disconnected surf of radio static, I ask Lionel if he was able to get the item that he promised to bring today.

"Patience is divine, Wheeler," he tells me, tilting his knobby head. His maverick wink says yes, he has brought the highly experimental drug that he promised he would bring, but that he is also going to proudly be a pain in the neck about it. I follow him to the car and sit in the backseat, among crumpled fast food sacks, and give the brooding, unspeaking Brooke directions on the mazey park roads to the pond where the rangers never stop. In the front seat Lionel fast-forwards through the new Fishbone cassette, looking for a part of a song that he feels is currently the best expression of young black anger.

We are only young and angry, I point out. Not black.

"Two out of three ain't bad," Lionel mocks, in a dull voice. He knows his theories precisely, like inventions left lying around his personal laboratory. "That kind of thinking isn't going to bring people together, Wheeler."

Though everything's changed since Brooke drove him to my house two months ago, I've come to feel that it always goes this way, me in the backseat staring out the window, while Brooke drives and Lionel sits shotgun, pontificating in his small cutting voice. It's hard to keep in mind all that's changed, except that two months ago I wouldn't have considered smoking crystal-form cocaine. The word "crack" belonged to undead grown-ups that herded in unnamed ghettoes and to the straight-up cops who hunted them.

Lionel sometimes remarks, *How quickly and cruelly the outer world relates to you.* At times I have replied, *How quickly, Lionel? How cruelly?* and at others, *Lionel, could you relate that to Shut the fuck up.* More and more lately, I've been saying, *Yes, yes, how quickly indeed.* When we left my dad behind and came to the park, my mom tried to convince me of our safety here. "Things are going to get a lot easier," she used to say. "You're not going to believe it." She was looking out into the woods, reading about the school system. All along the cancer was inside her.

It's not saying I'm bitter, like kids they make TV movies about, just that I'm feeling open to a new way of living, a new way of thinking, once Brooke parks the Stingray on the broken-up black-top beside a long-unrented cottage of decaying logs, once we are climbing from two open doors into the sweet pungent autumn with instantly cold throats. Beyond our clouds of breath, a single fisherman sits in a lawn chair down on the dock with his line out in the dark pond, a bobber among the reflections and moss and leaves. It's Fritz, the harmless, muttering old German who catches and releases the sunfish and bluegill that otherwise have the run of this body of water. He wears a thermal flannel shirt and a hunter's cap and smokes a corncob pipe.

Brooke fears rangers, jails, courtrooms, and parents. Before the pregnancy she dated the quarterback of the football team. She sold brownies at the bake sale and wore glitter lipstick. She shivers and hugs herself in her thin suede jacket, and I stand beside her to murmur that all will be fine. This forest is my area of expertise. Lionel strides on ahead of us, stubby arms swinging, no jacket for him, into the opening in the trees that we have gone into many times before to drink Old Milwaukee and smoke the occasional joint. This is a special occasion, how-ever—momentous is the word, really—and my fear is gone now that I know for sure that Brooke, being with child, will say no to smoking crystal-form cocaine. If my mom had smoked crystal-form cocaine while she carried me, I don't know what I'd tell people.

We linger, she short and delicate in a way that makes me hide my hands in the kangaroo pouch of my hooded sweatshirt.

"What if he sees us?" she hisses.

"Don't worry. He's just this old guy." My whisper does not con-vince her, and she only follows so as not to be left alone with the half-blind old man sitting with his back to her, once I've almost disappeared from her sight down the trail into the leafless dog-woods—she catches up at a stumbling, paranoid jog. It's embar-rassing to see an older girl unnerved, so I don't mention to her that when I look back Fritz has turned in his chair to watch her through his thick bifocal glasses, chewing the pipe with his old teeth. I look a second longer to make sure he doesn't feel ignored by me, until he jerks a nod. Maybe a long time ago in the Black Forest or wherever, kids would meet in the woods to get it on. I go after Brooke, a step behind her, into the den of leafless branches, with my head down.

Our spot is a flat dry bank between an isolated chunk of gran-ite and a bald cypress. Lionel crouches on the boulder. He hops down as we squeeze through the branches of young basswoods. He pulls a small pipe from one pocket, from the other a small bag of dope and a little smoked glass vial that I recognize as having contained pure caffeine at one time in a cabinet in our General Science classroom. The day Mr. Clayborn got that stuff out so we could estimate its melting point, boys from our class stole them to flash such vials in the corridor and joke that they contained what Lionel's actually does. Explaining that he's already broken up the crystal, he twists off the lid and shakes frosty nuggets onto the swirl of twiggy pot in his bowl. Observing ritual, he balances the pipe on the toe of an Airwalk and searches out his cigarettes in the vast pockets of his jeans. "Wheeler?" He offers one, totally solemn, and I take it, light it, and pull out the bottle of apple-flavored wine I have stolen, smuggled, and hidden in my shirt as a surprise for my friends on this occasion.

"Thank God," says Brooke. She uncaps the bottle and drinks from it, watching Lionel and me smoke our Camels. "You guys are fucking crazy," she tells us between slugs, eyeing the pipe balanced like a hacky sack on Lionel's shoe. "That stuff can make your heart explode. What if you get addicted?"

"Then we get addicted." Lionel glares at her like she's his little sister, whom he had no choice but to bring along this one time. I happen to know that he loves her and wants to adopt the baby when she has it. He tells me all his secrets and thoughts. He imagines putting the baby into a car seat once he's got his license. He says he sees them moving into a slab house in his neighborhood together. He'll be a construction worker, come home to her in the evenings. Then I'll stop by, and we'll drink beer in the living room. Lionel believes his love is all the more legit because Brooke annoys him — this time because he has conducted actual research on this particular chemical under the reading lamps at the downtown library, and he is confident that the first-timer-hooked story is falderal meant to deter us from passing into an alternate world that could lead to a higher reality. This higher reality stuff isn't very clear to me.

"That's the problem," he says. "The way the system is set up. So you won't see that every second is another chance to shoot into another dimension."

Lionel winks at Brooke, then takes the first hit, mouth puckered hard around the piece, holds it and blushes, and quilts my face with pot smoke. With a hurry-up motion he hands me the pipe, and then, with an audible heartbeat and damp armpits, I'm doing it myself, staring directly into the disapproval of too-thin, pretty if slightly buck-toothed Brooke.

A ball of tension in my chest releases into a greater tightness that makes me understand for the first time that my mind is a part of my physical body. There I am, standing on taut legs, laughing with Lionel, as Brooke freaks out and drinks green wine from the bottle, the three of us on the mud bank of a still pond under a spry autumn cloud.

This is all that happens.

As far as I know.

That makes me laugh like I've never laughed before, so hard I think I'll break my chest, and Lionel walks up with a cackle in his throat and punches me in the cheek. I bop him in the middle of his bald head and he goes down, laughing, on the hard bank. We sit together, painless, sharing a pipe, and drum our legs on the bank. Brooke calls us idiots, but more importantly, the autumn is its naked self, bold and inelegant, and hard like a new tooth driven through a baby's gums. We laugh hard and cry and get scared and laugh hard, and Brooke stares at the pond and shakes her head, drinking wine and being pregnant.

On our last night together my dad stands in the red bathroom with my mom's hair in his fist. He uses his knuckles to point her eyes directly into the toilet. He shouts in a voice torn down to a squeak, that she has to take the fucking cabbage out of the fucking toilet. This during the period we believe that alcohol does this to him. The toilet is empty. Nonetheless my mom, wide-eyed in pain and by now done talking to him, lowers both hands in, hoping, I guess, to catch my dad's hallucination in both her palms as she lifts them out. She tries not to get the floor too wet.

After he passes out I climb out from under their bed, from under his flung out arms and the broad shining slope of his belly. My mom has been preparing for this, and the duffel bags are out of the closet. She composes her clothes and hair enough to go outside, composes her head enough to drive the car. She kneels beside me, and we look at the snoring, slobbering disaster that is my dad. She breathes hard and I breathe hard and we both smell like the kind of tears that don't mean anything, the useless tears that continue to fall after the reasons for the pain are isolated and as uninteresting as childhood toys.

We drive to the house of a friendly ranger my mom knows. We stay in his stone cottage less than two miles away, but I don't see my dad again until we go to the courthouse. He wears a suit, his face sickly white-and-yellow, his guido hair combed back. Except for the tattoo of a five-pointed star on his right ear, he does not resemble the oaf who raged in our house throwing unbreakable plastic dinnerware and glassless photographs and tackling heavy wooden chairs, searching for nonexistent friends and sometimes naked when he'd fabricated a coyly hiding lover. In the court he is frightened and sick, as the clerk reads from my mother's testimony about some things he's done, which I remember well, which he says he does not remember. He scares me most like this, braced in agony, without his usual, unkind happiness.

A psychiatrist questions him for a week and takes pictures of his brain that are blown up and colored for the benefit of the judge and lawyers. He is diagnosed as schizophrenic, and when they tell him this in the courtroom he weeps. He has not had alcohol to drink for almost a month by now. Lighter and sweaty and shivering, he stutters when he tries to talk after the judge asks if he has anything to say.

He looks at us at our little table, me in my suit and tie, and says, "I-I-'m s-s-s-sorr-ry," as if he has eaten a speech therapy student, who is speaking from inside his stomach.

My mom maintains an upright posture in her gray suit, her face smart and ready. She is nearly free, and looking past the present, she hardly knows he is there.

They move my dad into an institution in the farmlands north of Lima, Ohio, but he doesn't know where it is. He doesn't know that we move east along the lake, not because he's vindictive and murderous but because he takes Thorazine. He can't keep drool in his mouth.

I don't miss him. In six years I'll take an unannounced trip to Lima over Christmas break, in an '89 Accord, and be informed by a doctor there of my dad's release after three years due to cuts in hospital funding. My mom will apologize for not telling me. She will be forty-one and still bald, and it will be easy to forgive her. When I drop out of college that spring I'll drive to Panama City, where he's thought to have gone in search of a climate conducive to heavy drinking and homeless living. After a week of talking to volunteers in missions around the city, I'll be directed to a block near Buccaneer stadium, and he'll be the old man in mesh shorts sitting in the shade of a viaduct. The star on his grimy ear will look like a tattoo of used chewing gum. I won't know if he knows me, but like I think we're bros, I'll buy two forties and sit with him. After saying a few planned things, I give him my goddamn beer and leave him there.

This is what happens in Mr. Clayborn's General Science for Freshmen, a boring required course in which I fail to foresee an oncoming disaster. In this class students sit in pairs at green Formica lab tables, and since Lionel and I are lab partners and contemptuous of our childish peers, we sit together and sneer at our surroundings. Our table is in the back corner beside a cabinet in which a pig fetus, a pine rattlesnake, a mudpuppy, and a cow's heart float in jars of formaldehyde. In the larger cabinet behind us are stored seriously unstable compounds and elements, all of them in smoked glass jars. Several times per class period, Lionel and I wish they would explode. Lionel is one of three Advanced Chemistry students in the freshmen class, and as far as we know he is the only one who's noticed this powder keg in the classroom. Today we feel especially superior, fourteen-year-olds who have smoked crystal-form cocaine and survived without becoming addicted to it. Every few minutes I write into Lionel's notebook: *You a fiend yet?*

"No," he whispers.

How about now? I write.

"Not yet."

Today Mr. Clayborn lugs in a large cardboard box containing his taxidermic collection of roadkill. Mr. Clayborn, PETA member, boombox-toting founder of Right Now!, faculty advisor to the freshman class president, master of the a.m. glad-handed greeting, how we scorn you. You and your box of preserved armadillo, jackrabbit, chipmunks, guinea fowl, raccoon, and squirrels. Lionel and I are cool as gargoyles as our classmates express chirpy excitement about today's plan to pass around animal corpses.

Mr. Clayborn's nose wrinkles as he breathes through his mouth, out of breath and flushed from the exertion of carrying these dead animals up two flights of stairs, a light fog in his glasses. "I thought you guys might want to get a good look at an armadillo's feet."

Lionel opens a turquoise folder and mutters into it, "I thought you might want to get a good look at my balls."

Mr. Clayborn holds up the small, armored, pig-faced animal so that we can see its wicked-looking black claws. "This guy is my favorite. It's truly a wonder that such a timid beast is endowed with such dangerous natural tools." It is this verbal excess that pushes Lionel into the airless realm of disbelief. On the desk he tilts our worksheet that features diagrams of the animals in Clayborn's box. He scribbles neat, elaborate notes in the margins with a number 2 pencil. By the time the armadillo reaches our table we have thoroughly studied, written about, and added genitals to diagrams of the jackrabbit, the squirrels, and the raccoon. All of the lab groups are working at what Mr. Clayborn deems a medium noise level. I am well-informed of what Lionel expects of me, and I wait until a girl in the front asks a complicated question and Clayborn is preoccupied.

I'm nervous, and Lionel is right there beside me, urging through thin, excited lips, "Do it, Wheeler, do it, get us in trouble. You think you know how much but you never will if you don't do it." With a newly sharpened pencil he traces a five-pointed star in the middle of our worksheet until the paper tears. "Come on, come on."

As Mr. Clayborn explains a squirrel's digestive system to a pair of girls up front, I take the shiny armadillo in both hands. It's light and hollow and football-sized. I pretend to weigh my options, letting Lionel's words tickle until I can no longer control myself. I twist off its claws quickly and, snickering, hand it to Lionel, who breaks into hard laughter at Mr. Clayborn's alarmed shout. As the teacher rushes to us, slamming hips against tables, Lionel drives his pencil up into the armadillo as far as it will go. He holds it up by the eraser, offering it like a Popsicle, and Mr. Clayborn swats it out of his hand so that it hits the floor and cracks.

"Oh my God," Brooke says as we wait in the long line of cars leaving the parking lot. She quickly smokes, trying to ignore the faces of her old schoolmates as they walk past us to their parked cars. She tells us, "You guys are assholes, in addition to being idiots."

Behind the rebukes she is amused, holding back a smile, and I think that perhaps she is baiting Lionel, to get him to joke with her. She's not used to him being such a grouch. It almost makes me talkative, but I don't want to get involved in their relationship. Except for the grunt with which he confirmed my story, he has made no sound since getting into the smoke-smelling car. He ignores her and holds his eyes on the blasted sky, and Brooke gives up on him for the moment.

We wait in full sight of her old friends and the quarterback ex-boyfriend she blames for her predicament. They stand in a stylish group beside the tennis courts, staring as we roll past, and the quarterback ex-boyfriend will not take his eyes off of Brooke holding the steering wheel and staring ahead. He's hoping she will let him look into her eyes, and then talk to her for just a minute, put his hand near hers, and so on. Brooke is strong under this pressure. She finds me in the rearview and asks about the headlines of the school paper, whether the editors are holding up without her.

The quarterback ex-boyfriend stops trying to get her attention and fumes at Lionel. Either Lionel doesn't notice, or he doesn't care. I worry about all this. This quarterback ex-boyfriend will stare all the way across the cafeteria at the empty table that Lionel and I share at lunch. I am bigger than he is, yet the flawless muscular black boys from the football team follow him like a bodyguard, and like the other white kids in this school I fear these stronger, handsomer black boys. But the quarterback ex-boyfriend's anger with Lionel is undercut by his ex-boyfriend sadness. I've been by his locker, and there are pictures of him with Brooke taped all over the door. At the moment I passed, two of Brooke's old friends were comforting him as he moped. Lionel says he is a pussy. It is not Brooke's quarterback ex-boyfriend that has made Lionel sit like a stony god of hatred in the front seat.

"Lionel, what's up with you today?" Brooke is cautious with him, asking gently, then respecting his silence as we escape the school grounds and cross the road where the subdivisions end and the farmlands begin on the way to the lakeshore.

Lionel will not admit that Clayborn caught him tongue-tied in the principal's office. It's too embarrassing for him. I don't like to think about it, but the truth is that Mr. Clayborn turned out to be tougher than we'd expected. He knows what Lionel and I are about, the ideas we have, even the way we view the teachers. Neither of us was prepared for this revelation. We could only dodge his eyes and listen. He sat on the edge of the principal's desk, as the principal supported him by repeatedly looking at us and then at his wristwatch. He pointed a thick Clayborn finger at each of us, one at a time. "This alternative education you're investing yourselves in isn't going to pay off, unless you guys are trying to find out what the floor smells like in Stryker, because that's where this kind of behavior is going to take you." He said this to both of us but the conversation was between him and Lionel. And when Lionel opened his mouth, Mr. Clayborn cut him off. "What do you think, that nobody's done any of this stuff before? You think you're Butch Cassidy and the Sundance Kid."

"He doesn't even know what he's saying," Lionel tells Brooke and me, as he and I prepare to smoke more crystal-form cocaine and disappoint Brooke, in our spot. "He couldn't possibly understand the subtlety of our project." He does not attempt to explain this subtlety. It seems best not to ask him to. We all three sit against the granite hunk because Fritz the German lunatic has moved from his usual place on the dock and relocated directly across the murky water from us, shrunk by a hundred yards' distance, and though I don't think he can see that far I'm not very comfortable with the possibility. Even if we did not drink wine and beer and smoke cigarettes and crystal-form cocaine, I don't believe

I would want anyone to see the three of us out here. My friends don't embarrass me, but I'm not sure we'll always be friends.

Lionel produces a spike of fire with his butane lighter and sparks a bowl. He exhales and gives me the pipe, then lays back against the boulder with his arms relaxed at his sides. Like a toy bald person. His chest rises and falls faster, and he grins his cottonmouth grin and tells us, "Yes. Fuck Clayborn. I'll kick his ass with thoughts."

I'm slow to smoke and I hold the pipe to my lips awhile. Brooke has developed a small double chin, which Lionel and I agree is very cute. She hides her pregnant belly under sweatshirts and coats, though Lionel has touched her bare skin and felt the baby kick. He tells me she would let me do this as well, that it's not a couples thing, but I said no thanks. I'm not interested in touching her, or in babies. She smokes and blows rings, pensive and sad and resigned to look over at us for a reason to smile, and she sees me holding the pipe like I am. She rolls her eyes.

"You two," she says, and looks away. It is as if we have once again caused her to catch us wearing her bras on our heads, and it is no longer funny. In a way we have come to enjoy this general feeling. I light up and enjoy what's left of the day in this season of diminishing afternoons. It's cold with a gonna-storm dampness, and we are all three in jackets beside the pond full of sunken leaves.

Lionel believes that Brooke is tougher than either of us. He tells me this as we smoke cigarettes under the clean autumn night sky. He is thinking about their future together, which is what he thinks about when Brooke is gone and he is tired of thinking about getting even with Mr. Clayborn.

Today Brooke went to a sonogram reading with her quarterback ex-boyfriend and all their parents. Strictly political. She disobeys her parents most of the time and does what she wants to but says they deserve to have a daughter once in a while. "So much wiser than us," says Lionel, a little high from this afternoon. "She's *tough*."

I'm inclined to agree with him.

When the school nurse interpreted the blue plus sign on the home test for her, Brooke knew she was as good as expelled. She pulled off her senior class ring and squeezed it in her fist until she felt sweat or blood. That summer she could get an equivalent degree and depart from her academic days in virtual obscurity, without throwing a mortarboard or a party in her parents' backyard. She wanted none of it, nor did she want the words being said by the young nurse sitting beside her on the tightly made white cot.

The nurse, a graduate of a women's college who trusted her youthful sensibilities to overlap with ours, was saying a lot of words, and one especially. Options.

Brooke pushed the hand from her elbow and walked out of the office. She took the dizzy road to her boyfriend's chemistry class where, between teacher and chalk equations and twenty-two concentrating adolescents, everyone knew something had gone wrong. A few kids later bragged that they had guessed she was knocked up, but no one claimed to have the intuition to predict her next move. No one would have believed that story, because we all knew that people would meet up years later and still express excitement and surprise over the new confidence that she displayed as she lifted her quarterback boyfriend's pen hand by the wrist and confiscated his highlighter and then planted her sweaty ring in the center of his palm.

It was the twin of his, and he had paid for both. To wear them had been his idea, like they were teenagers and tacky and also engaged, and Brooke wanted no more reminders.

With the ring in his hand her quarterback boyfriend became her ex. People said he was totally still and that he didn't lift his head until she'd turned away. Now that she'd done what she came to do, Brooke's strength began to leave her, her shoulders fell, and she rushed toward the classroom door, almost tripped, then disappeared clattering into the hall. The class sat stunned through the long, shrill bell.

I wonder what she does all day while we sit at school. When I ask Lionel, he tells me, "Stuff that pregnant dropouts do." It troubles him, too, the mystery of her. Moonlight falls blue on his head as he smokes and thinks of her, off with the strangers she knows.

I imagine her routine involving a quart of mint chocolate chip ice cream, a television, and all the sadness that a person by herself can work up. Maybe Brooke and my mom watch the same programs while I'm at school all day. Maybe they could get together, get their schedules lined up.

My mom is called to the school the day that Lionel sets off the explosions in the senior bathroom. This is after the paramedics rush six football players out of the school on gurneys, Brooke's quarterback ex-boyfriend among them, sitting up in goony anguish over the terrible bleeding burn on his throwing hand.

I walk into the principal's office, escorted by two city cops who are good at scowling. There's my mom, sitting across the desk from the principal and Mr. Clayborn. She has put on jeans and pulled a pink T-shirt over a thermal undershirt, beneath which she wears a bra that reproduces the bulge of breasts. She is wearing the wig of bouncy blonde-brown hair that she hates like a curse put on her alone. By the light glaze on her blue eyes I see that she had not planned to leave the house today. She has a hard time keeping her head still and probably wants to take a nap. When the principal voices concern that she might pass out, she holds up a bony hand and says, "Huh-uh." She reaches out her shaking hand for me, and I sit facing her so that she can try to pulverize my shoulder with her weak grip.

"You," she says, almost as tall as me but oh so brittle. "Did you do this?"

"No." I didn't. It was the first of our experiments for which I was demoted to observer status. Lionel didn't trust me to handle the potassium hydroxide. He thought I'd bring it into contact with a microscopic piece of water, and so he dried the sinks in the bathroom himself, stuffed the drains with paper towels, and then sprinkled into each a few white crystalline flakes. The potassium hydroxide flakes resembled the crystal-form cocaine that we have smoked in our spot near my house. Lionel dismissed my analogy with a callous bah-and-wave. He peeled off latex gloves and said, "If you want to smoke it, I suggest you wear a gas mask."

I had only meant that there was perhaps a noticeable cycle in our experiments. My point was lost, in the gloom of the bathroom, on his single celebration bounce. He led me out into the hall, where we hung out next to a window with the view of the lot of gleaming student cars and waited for lunch to end and the football team to trash the senior bathroom, according to routine. As they roared past us into the brick-walled lavatory, none of them noticed us, except for the quarterback ex-boyfriend, that melancholy ad model whose diminishing power was to make you feel sorry for him. He moped at us, and we stared at him, invincible nobodies. As the daily riot started inside, Lionel and I headed for the doors to the gym hallway, for we were scheduled to be physically educated.

The first bang sounded just as we reached the end of the lockers. It was as if a big, steel pocket of air had burst, followed by shouts in the bathroom, the sounds of boys directing one another in matters of first aid. We stopped. Someone shouted some nonsense about a gun, and girls began to scream from the bathroom down to our end of the corridor. The second explosion sent us all running out of the school, Lionel and me at the front of a teeming mob of panicked teenagers. He was trying very hard to laugh at what he had done, but like me he grew quiet once we stood behind the fearful, gossiping, overreacting crowd in the parking lot.

For some time he looked down at his Airwalks, and then, as if something had occurred to him, his face hardened like that of a guy going out to the firing squad. He took his cigarettes from his pocket and lighted one. There was nothing he could do, now that he had done what he had done. Suspicions about his involvement were only as natural to the principal and Mr. Clayborn, the keeper of volatile chemicals, as was their dislike of a kid who shaved his head and wore pictures of zombies on his shirts and who sneered at them with all the calculated ferocity of a fourteen-year-old. Lionel was who he was, and I admired him for it. He sighed and wearily smiled and looked over the crowd and the school like he owned both. He smoked an illicit cigarette on school grounds, knowing he would be lucky to finish it before they marched out to seize him. I looked across the heads of the crowd to the shining school doors, where there appeared, no mistake, Mr. Clayborn, who immediately saw me, the marker of Lionel's location.

Clayborn was not graceful in his apprehension of my friend. The cigarette fell to the blacktop and continued to burn, as its owner was dragged off by a nearly violent science teacher into the crowd of impressed students. I was surprised to be left standing alone, but the students were watching Lionel. It was as if I, the biggest freshman in the school, had somehow been overlooked.

I went in with the crowd when the fire trucks left and attended what was left of gym class. No one bothered to change for the few minutes left, and we were shooting around in our school clothes when the cops came into the gymnasium and asked Ms. Nagle which kid was me.

Expecting to be handcuffed for the first time in my life, I tell Mr. Clayborn and the principal that I am not responsible for the chemical mines. They confer, and Mr. Clayborn suggests that I wouldn't have known about these compounds. "He's not in the advanced class with Lionel. And I just don't think Francis would do something like this."

To my disbelief and great guilt they believe me. My mom is willing to let them believe what they want to. She has her own plans for me. The principal sends the policemen away. I am told that as we speak Lionel is waiting to be taken to jail. The principal and Mr. Clayborn are oddly compassionate as they tell me this. They treat me like an old friend, and I squirm in my chair. From these men I expected nothing less than persecution and torture. For some reason they now view me with eager curiosity in their middle-aged faces.

From his perch on the desk, Mr. Clayborn says, "I know that you went along with him because you didn't want him to feel alone. I understand. He's a bright kid, and it must have hurt him to be wrong about a lot of things. Why was he so unhappy? Was it his family?"

Who can say? A fourteen-year-old boy, no matter how tall and physically mature, cannot. My mom is one person in the room who is aware of this.

"I'm going to take him home now," she says. She's exhausted, and these men are crazy to her. At the door she tells them, "Lionel was his best friend."

She's driven the cruiser and I sit shotgun, trying to see into the backseats of the police cars parked along the curb ahead of us for Lionel's bald head.

"They already took him away," my mom says, as she starts the engine and puts the car into motion. The school is five stories, orange brick, looking down on a broad lawn with four black walnut trees and, across the highway, fallow soybean fields. Once, the sheer size of the building in the middle of this nothingness shocked me, as it does again now. I want to never go back. I want to run away or kill myself. I want an unimaginable fate to lie in store for me at home. As we get farther away from the school, driving in silence, these things become less and less likely.

When we've gone a mile or so she switches on the radio and sings along with some band of whiners from the sixties. Her voice is soft and harsh, but she can bellow when she feels like it. Great, I think, sing me to death. I have a sour mouth. I realize that I know this song. I've sung it before, with my mom, on the road. She turns to me, slowly saying the words as though to remind me of what they are, though she knows that I do. It's not okay to laugh, even though she's teasing me. What am I going to do? Pout? I give it up, lie back in my seat, and sing along.

That afternoon I don't know what to do with myself, and I sit on my front porch smoking cigarettes and checking to make sure my mom isn't moving around downstairs. I'm not in trouble, just brought home early, cautioned. I'm sitting on the flagstone front porch, paranoid, Camel to my lips, when Brooke pulls into the driveway.

She is glassy-eyed and grimacing, more unhappy than I've seen her. I worry she's abandoned Lionel and gone back to her quarterback ex-boyfriend. She mentions none of this, just says that she wants me to come with her out to our spot. On the way she bitches about how stupid it was of Lionel to try to kill her quarterback ex-boyfriend (for this is how she interprets his act) and then to get caught doing it.

"What's he trying to do?" she asks. "Punish me by taking all the men out of my life?" She is through with men, she says; she will become a born-again virgin and live in France as a nun.

We weave fast through the stripped trees, and I look out for rangers and hope against a second encounter with the authorities in a single day. Not soon enough we are parked, and she is slamming out of the car, cussing out the gray disturbance in the sky, telling Fritz the crazy and now startled fisherman that he can go fuck himself too, and then running down the leaf-covered trail to the boulder, with me jogging in pursuit.

She stands at the edge of the pond and utters a valedictory to love and life as she knows it, and reaches into her purse and brings out Lionel's pipe, wrapped in tissue. She has it ready to smoke, and preserved this way, packaged, rubber-banded tight. "I've decided to kill the baby," she tells me, theatrical and self-pitying.

Of course, she's been trying to kill the baby since I met her.

"Oh for the love of Pete, don't stand there!" she shouts at me in disbelief. "Come take this thing away from me."

I do this, look at the packed bowl, a real winner, and put it in my pocket. Later I'll trash it. Crystal-form cocaine is not something I want to be smoking by myself.

Brooke sniffs and dangles a crushed pack of cigarettes. "These, too."

I store these with the drugs.

"Anything else you'd like to give me?" I ask.

Brooke surrenders a miniature bottle of Jack Daniels. She sighs and cocks her head at me, dainty but for her protuberant belly under her gray peacoat. She's out of tears and anger, and I can see that she's done what she's come here to do. I guess she's making a lot of quick adjustments now that Lionel's in trouble. In irony I offer her my arm. She takes it, and we walk this way to the clearing, to her car.

Fritz is standing at the end of the dock, his pole beside his mucky galoshes. He's got this big painter turtle in his hands.

Brooke stops. "What is it?" she asks.

"Ach," says Fritz, holding his rod to the dock with a galosh. He's biting down on his fishing line, keeping it taut so the turtle's head stays out of its shell. Its neck fully extended, the turtle frantically paws the air.

The line falls out of his teeth, and Fritz roars at the turtle, "What are you doing awake?" The turtle's head goes into its shell, and Fritz's throat catches like he's going to get upset.

I go over and take the line, and standing over the old man's uneasy breathing, I sort of pull the turtle's head out of its shell with the line. The poor animal's wrinkly neck is taut and it hisses at me, but Fritz says not to worry, I won't break it.

"I'm going to go, Wheeler. I'm going to leave you here." Brooke pouts on her way to the driver's side. I wave okay and stand closer to Fritz to help him get the hook out of the poor turtle's beak. It upsets Brooke that I do not chase her, and she sits a moment in her car, watching us, furious and prettier that way, in black eyeliner.

"My friend is in love with that girl," I tell Fritz.

Fritz says, "That girl is a bitch. Eiskalt. Your friend is a scheisse."

I don't argue with people who are insane or old. It turns out I can hold the turtle's mouth open with a key as the old fisherman pulls the hook from the upper part of its beak, chipping it, but getting it out of there. The car starts and kicks up gravel. Fritz and I look over, and Brooke is staring straight at me, a second before she drives out of my childhood. There's an understanding of this between the three of us, before it slips out to a place beyond words, and she squeals her tires.

"There we are," says Fritz, "good as new. Almost."

I step away, and he releases the turtle into the cold autumn water.

From that moment I know Brooke won't come to my house again by herself. As it will turn out, she will never return to the house where I stay the next four years with my mother. Lionel will be released from the Child Study Institute when he is eighteen, and we will not resume our friendship. By then Brooke will have a daughter and be married to her disfigured quarterback ex-boyfriend. Lionel will swear off terrorism and go live in some mountains somewhere to write poems for kids. Sad local Christians will put him in their newspaper, and I'll read the article about his struggles and poverty and his vision of peace-loving kids. An hour later I won't be able to recall any of it verbatim.

I will hear of Brooke's divorce in another city, and after I have forgotten about it, I will come into the watery state of the present moment, being twenty-three years old, a door-to-door book salesman passing through Missouri. I am the weirdo on the doorstep, the ogre in the trenchcoat, leather attaché in hand, preposterous, quoting Faust to housewives.

"A man is being made," I tell them, accept their rejections, and traipse away across their dry autumn yards.

At a house in the suburbs, Brooke answers the door, older, sturdier. An attractive woman with a serious life, or at least she dresses this way. We share surprise, silence, and nervous laughter. We find we are happy to see one another. Each of us is happy to see how well the other has survived. There is an offer of coffee in the wood-paneled dining room. An introduction to the little girl spying on us from the kitchen doorway. Auburn pigtails a mess, the emcee of the great room. Through the passageway I see there are toys scattered across the white carpet—the plastic castle and the pretend-beach of naked, sunbathing dolls, beside the many pages of blue construction paper that Brooke explains make up the broad and deep Pacific Ocean.

I think it for an instant only, but Brooke perceives my flinch. Our chatter fails as the daughter she once forsook for two months comes into the room, sensing something wrong, and wants to sit on her mother's lap. She is too big for this and sits there blocking Brooke's mouth, furious at my intrusion, shoulders hunched up beneath her tiny ears.

I want to tell Brooke what Lionel once advised me, that when you remember something you're not proud of, it's best to think of the outcome as inevitable. It helps to pass the memory, he said. Instead I finish my coffee. Brooke sees me to the front door without the pretense of a smile, and we resume being the people we tell ourselves we are.

AFTER THE FLOOD

✧

The Mississippi swells up and covers the town and the surrounding forest, devastating all visible creation. Hundreds of egrets fly north; there is no counting the dead. The steeple of St. Francis of Assisi marks the submerged churchyard of obelisks, crosses, and angels. Broken boats and tables drift under convulsing clouds stitched up with lightning. There will be no going back from this deluge, no recovery of the lost civilization, no afterward. With his thoughts clear now, when actions matter, Daniel Gauthier pilots the auto ferry across churning brown currents, collecting survivors. His gray hair blows, and the waters drown his shouts as he pulls families from rooftops, men and women clinging to furniture, a girl shivering at the top of a pine. Townsfolk crowd the concrete deck, facing the horizon, straining for a glimpse of solid earth.

A knocking at the window wakes him from his recurrent dream. At first he's disappointed, a dried-up mansion of the past, an aging man who fits the ruts of his empty bed. His words jumble when he sees the dark face in the pane, then converge in a groan as he recognizes the profile and frown of Sheriff Charlie Boudreaux. Unable to comprehend why his onetime friend has trampled his peonies at 2:32 in the morning, he lifts the window and blinks several times, in the place of a what-the-hell kind of question.

The sheriff eases out of the flower bed, whispering, "Come out here, Daniel. First you better look in on that boy."

Minutes later the men share a front seat like they haven't in years, only now it's a police cruiser and not a truck recently resurrected on cinder blocks. When they reach the Kelly plantation the sheriff parks by a row of gardenias, where they can see the moonstruck white house through an alley of live oaks. Daniel broods quietly while the sheriff, sensing his ire, takes an apologetic tone. Someone has put the torch to four plantation houses in as many weeks, and not half an hour ago the sheriff saw a first-story light blink on and in the window, briefly, Daniel's unhappy stepson, Clive. Aware of Clive's records as a juvenile and adult felon, and how the newspapers would make the confused kid out to be a villain, Charlie Boudreaux suggests that maybe someone else struck the matches at the other fires. "He's snooping around in there, probably."

"Dumbshit's probably looking for something to pawn," Daniel croaks, not wanting to admit his fear that Clive is using the mansion as a flophouse. His combination of logic and grouchiness satisfies the sheriff, whose loyalties to friend and to city compromise each other. The Kelly family hired Clive to clear the weeds from their garden and cut the lawn, not to clean the house. Before they left for the summer they told him to stay outside unless there was an emergency. They left a copy of these instructions with the sheriff's office. Charlie Boudreaux should go in there and arrest Clive, but Daniel knows the man he called his best friend for more than half his days won't do that.

They see Clive's flashlight beam touch a window on the third floor. A minute later they spy the same light on the floor below. The sheriff sighs and looks at his steering wheel. "If I called it in they'd think the kid burned them other houses. I mean I've seen Clive around town. He moves like somebody beat him in the back of a truck going sixty and then threw him out the back. He's not the destructive kind, not anymore. But those people will think what they want."

"He's mentally a child. He missed more of a decade of growing up because he was getting stoned. Basically he was switched off."

"That's the reason I came to you."

"Thanks, Charlie. I'll go get him."

"Promise me it won't happen again, Daniel."

Daniel can't promise what another person will or won't do, least of all his troubled stepson, who's recently come home after twelve years away, with a set of yolky eyes he developed by shooting New Orleans heroin into his veins. His pocked forearms look sprayed with birdshot, a record of compulsive behavior that one day convinced Daniel to copy the keys to the Kelly mansion while Clive showered.

Daniel promises the sheriff that his stepson won't trespass in the house again, having no other way to get out of the cruiser without a disquisition on free will. In the yard he ducks a bush to be startled by a white statue, a naked youth reaching out an open hand to the stars, or maybe the figure has flung them up there. Through the shrills of the cicadas comes a panther shriek, far away and quick, like a girl gladly frightened, and Daniel catches his breath. He knows that big cat, drove up on it once on the side of the road, where it cringed in his pickup truck's headlights. So near he could've blasted it with the shotgun he keeps behind the seat. Since the panther eats local house cats, killing it would have made him a local hero. The thought never crossed his mind as he admired the crouching feline, who let Daniel see his teeth. Years ago, men from the state brought them in vented trucks from Florida and loosed them in the woods to prey on feral pigs. Now folks want the big cats dead, too, and these days they're rare. Daniel laid on his horn and frightened the panther into the woods.

He lets himself into the Kelly mansion's carpeted entrance hall, eyes peeled for his stepson. He doesn't know what to expect from the twenty-nine-year-old, who talks and acts like a teenager, and he scans the floor for the silhouette of the overdosed. He knows the figure in his own bank account and guesses he can afford the rehab clinic, providing he can find Clive and get him out of here before a less charitable sheriff shows up.

"Clive," he says, his voice small in the darkness. "You in here?"

He's drawn by a lighted doorway into an old parlor. Electric lights reflect in a small crystal chandelier, and once bathed in the bleeding color of the yellow walls, he gazes out into the hall with the unreasonable fear that some phantom will leap out at him. There's a stairwell leading to the darkness upstairs.

"Clive?" He's reluctant to go up, even though Clive might be somewhere above his head, tying off this very moment. He looks over a row of dull Kelly portraiture and sees a player piano in one corner of the brightened room, its polished wood gathering dust. He flips a switch on its backside panel, and the keys begin to move, producing a doleful song he identifies as a hymn. He levers up the volume, trusting Clive, if he's still conscious, to hear the music and come downstairs. Daniel used to do this when he was dating Clive's mother, Lucy, and the boy would hide in the house. Daniel would be in his best suit and aftershave, Lucy in pearls with her hair up, and Clive would be hidden in a closet somewhere in the house. While Lucy clicked on her high heels from room to room, shouting her son's name, Daniel would pull a record from the bookshelf and play it on the hi-fi, sending a tune through the air and along the floorboards to wherever Clive lay, and telling the boy that the two of them were bound to one another in ways that transcended the visual world. After a minute or so, Clive would emerge, pleased with himself, and run to Daniel, in whose arms he was safe from his mother's spanking.

Daniel doesn't hug his stepson now that Clive's grown. He rarely touches anyone. People standing too close give him gooseflesh. In his pinstriped pajamas and scuffed workboots, he watches the stairwell, nervous about the dark still rooms around him and the low ceiling and close walls in this one. He lights a cigarette to make himself comfortable. All day up on the ferry's driving platform, in the high heat, these little rolls of tobacco make constant companions. He lights each new one with the cherry of the last.

Clive creaks down the steps like a sullen child. In the parlor he stops beside an old yellow globe, looking at brown and green countries and beige oceans rather than make eye contact with his stepfather. "How'd you know where I was?"

Daniel gives him an incredulous look, but Clive doesn't seem to have a sense of his own wrongdoing ingrained in that bowed head of his. The kid stands there, frowning at his shoes, waiting for instruction. Daniel wonders how quickly an addict's conscience breaks down when the need for oblivion kicks in. "I knew because you almost got arrested."

Clive swallows and glances up. Almost hopeful, he says, "Really?"

"You realize that there's someone running around setting fires in these houses? Are you awake when you're walking around? Do you know that someone is scaring the bejesus out of the good old boys? Are you functional?" Daniel's sure to be harsh. He wants a lesson to sink in. "Get out in the truck. You're giving me a ride home."

"You're wearing your pajamas," Clive tells him. Weary-eyed, shiftless with his thumbs in his back pockets, he obeys, almost tripping on the last step down. His disorderly gait reminds Daniel of himself as a youngster, though they don't share a drop of blood.

Daniel keeps a stern face as he follows the shamed young man through the balmy night to his truck. He's relieved when he's not questioned about getting in the front door and remembers what it is to be young and fear people of authority. Certain of their power, you enslaved yourself to them. Clive climbs up into the driver's seat and when he hesitates before unlocking the passenger-side door,

Daniel raps sharply on the window to keep him in the present. The cab reeks sharply, of what precisely, Daniel can't tell. He can't smell much of anything anymore, but that sense can be a curse here, in the land of paper mills and oil refineries. He lifts a cigarette to his dried lips.

"Don't light that," Clive says. He lowers his eyes and mumbles, "I spilled gas in here earlier. I'll clean it up in the morning."

"Unbelievable, Clive. You're lucky it was Charlie Boudreaux who caught you in there."

"I was just looking around."

"Better not be getting high in there."

"I haven't done anything but drink a few beers since you brought me back here," Clive says quietly, watching the road.

"Whatever you're doing, do it during the daytime, when it won't scare people. And don't think you can pawn a single silver spoon from that house. There's not an antique dealer in three hundred miles of here that won't know where it came from." Daniel watches his stepson steer them around bends in the forest highway. Clive's window is down, and crushed bugs accumulate on his bare arm. He takes no notice, as if, mentally, he's all horizontal skies interrupted by chaotic squiggles of thought. Daniel taps his cigarette back into the box, calculating he has less than two hours to sleep before the alarm clock on his dresser does its noisy dance. Above them, stars of varying brightness evoke the many ceilings of the night sky. Not a rain cloud in sight.

Clive left home at seventeen and spent twelve years in New Orleans, working the till in a voodoo shop near the river end of the Quarter to pay for his drug habit. Daniel and Lucy knew the location of the store, but they never visited the business when they drove down for a weekend or the odd day of drinking. At that point in time Lucy didn't want to see her son again.

She'd found him passed out on the bathroom floor, screamed unforgivable things at him, and seen him driven off by sheriffs too many times. She'd given up trying to make him behave. She said he could come home when he was ready. It seemed unjust to Daniel, whose father had been fond of saying that you knew who truly loved you by who fought back when they came to drag you off.

Once when they were a block away from Clive's place of employment, drinking margaritas in plastic cups and feeling young and loose-limbed, Daniel proposed they walk over to the tourist shop. He had collected an ad from a window, a slick pamphlet with a cartoon of a bloodshot eye on the front. Lucy puckered her lips and shook her head. Visiting that haunted city was her vacation, and if one of its ghosts belonged to her, it just made her that much realer. She shrugged off his suggestion, and the afternoon began to wind down. Daniel tried to imagine what his wife was thinking, holding her hand on the patio while they ordered another round and then another to reignite the dying day. Matching with eager nods and laughs the cheer she forced into her face and voice, he was sorry, devoting his affections entirely to her, damning himself. Lucy needed to free herself for an afternoon, to be nothing more than a woman in a city of hedonists, with a man at her side, a man who was him, after all. Maybe he'd never understood her in the first place, and when he insisted that he did she'd patted his hand. After that, he didn't mention Clive again. And then, after years of forgetting, after new reasons for grief replaced the old ones, the telephone rang, and when Daniel picked it up, Clive spoke to him from the other side. Though he hadn't thought of his stepson in years, though he no longer saw the face in the framed pictures he'd left hanging on the walls, though twelve years had made Clive a damaged man, Daniel knew the voice that spoke his name with trepidation. He knew that Clive was in trouble. There could be no other reason for the call. Though his obligations to his stepson had gone with Lucy, Daniel felt the boy's house all around him where now he, stepfather, outsider, lived alone. He wanted badly to tell Clive how sorry he was, to make up for what he felt he'd taken, which did not belong to him. On the other end of the line, Clive rambled on about an adrenalin shot, a mugging, an eviction, debt, his sick girlfriend. Both men comprehended that the other was overjoyed.

Daniel spoke with so much force that he silenced Clive. "Where are you? What is your exact location?" he said. "I'm going out to my truck right now. I'm coming to get you."

The long drive gave him time to reflect on living without family. His parents were gone, leaving him with no one to visit, and he'd come to forget the dense familiarities of living in a house of people's habits. To walk into a living room and be at peace with the child sprawled out on the couch, rapping along with a music video. To find a woman in his bedroom, trying on earrings in her underwear. His days had grown so meager with what was not exactly asceticism and not exactly self-neglect that he worried he wouldn't know what to say when he found Clive and the girl he'd said would be with him. Living alone and working all week on the driving platform, he felt, had reshaped him into a subhuman creature, a being lean and smart and distrustful of folks, and he was ashamed of himself. He was sweating, speaking in a voice more boyish than the one he knew as his own, when he pulled up to the curb where Clive and Haley stood guard over two suitcases. He saw they were younger than he'd imagined, she even younger than Clive but just as worn down, and both of them tough in the way young people are, how they held their breath in and then spoke all at once, eager to impress him. They were just as nervous as he, and the ride home, three packed into the cab of his pickup, was just as silent as the drive down.

After coming back from the Kelly plantation, unable to sleep, Daniel thinks about these things and tries to reconstruct the events of the day, to figure out exactly why Clive was in that house. The kid didn't seem stoned, just confused, and the thought of the meek young man setting two-hundred-year-old houses on fire is too much a stretch of the familiar for his old mind to perform this late. He tries to remember whether he saw Clive this afternoon, after work, and he thinks maybe he did, though it could have been yesterday. Each day here feels the same, and between fixing things in the garage and driving that big orange barge back and forth across the river from five until three, he barely finds time to eat his supper, let alone babysit his stepson and Haley. They're grown-up, wayward perhaps, but not so much as others in town, the slobs on the roadhouse stools or the drones who surf the net all day at the public library. Sometimes Clive and Haley drive out of town at sunset to speed though the swamp woods in the dark in the red pickup he gave Clive as a homecoming gift. They don't go to the bars, not since Clive's second night back in Saintsville, when he got rolled over a pool table and thrown out into a gravel lot for saying the wrong thing to a deer hunter. Daniel thinks that they just go for long drives. That's what he did at their age. The cockleburs along the highway grew to your knee, and dead dogs lined the highway, and you just drove and drove, as if in search of a portal to someplace else. And after a while, it was like you'd found your way through, even though you were still rumbling around the coastal plain in your truck. He likes the thought of Clive and Haley cruising through the dark, young and pretty and too stupid to think beyond the easy intimacies at the disposal of all lovers. It reminds him of the good days with Lucy, before she got sick and he became the community recluse.

Comparing their love to the only one he's known, he lies on his side, worrying, until the birds chirping outside his window seem to multiply and the twilight creeps in.

He comes home that afternoon to hear them fighting about Clive's trespass into the Kelly mansion. Reluctant to involve himself in a passion he regards as personal, he waits on the porch, listening to Haley yell and Clive sneer back. Along the street, his neighbors take advantage of the evening cool, uprooting weeds from the flower beds, walking their dogs in the road. He knows their darting looks, the same ones they gave him at the council meeting where he refused to put a white picket fence around his yard despite the disdainful sniffs of the Historic Society. They stare at his dented black truck as if at ugly children hoping their imperfections will vanish overnight. The local fad has long been to drive a German car because pickups and souped-up racers line southern front yards, and rich people here pride themselves on their unique neighborhood. They love to step outside and see a bus parked at the end of the street and seventy senior citizens with cameras following a tour guide who knows more about their houses than they do. Lucy was one of these people, less a snob than most, but she still insisted on living in this house. Daniel keeps her silver BMW in the garage, in good condition, because he likes to have her old things around.

Clive slams out of the house and comes at him in an unintended gesture of challenge, then veers off, pouting, to sit on the porch swing. Daniel leans against a porch post and sighs, planning to avoid Haley by opening the garage door and resuming yesterday's project. He intends to replace the drive shaft in the outboard motor for the rowboat he never uses.

Through the screen door, Haley shouts, "Don't walk out on me. You think that'll shut me up. You jackass! They are going to put you in prison. I'm not going to be one of those women who visits." She steps out, prettier mad because her eyelashes seem longer, so slight her tank top wrinkles over her long denim skirt. Seeing Daniel, she grows quiet. "Hey."

"Hey," says Daniel, deducing that they could not have fought at any other time. Haley sleeps so heavily she wouldn't have stirred last night when Clive crawled into bed with her. His stepson leaves for work early, and if the weekends are any indication, most days she stays in bed until noon. Wanting last night to be over, forgotten, he looks at Clive. "You clean up the truck?"

Clive nods without looking up. His face sags from needing sleep.

"Thank you, Daniel, he means to say 'thank you.' He's so screwed up he forgot how to act to decent people." Haley folds her arms and gives her boyfriend an imperious look, which goes ignored, and Daniel guesses the fight is over. They won't fight in front of him, which is for the best, since the kinds of neighbors they have are the kind who like to eavesdrop and then invent stories to supplement the dialogue.

Though he listens at the supermarket and the post office and even eats in a couple of restaurants, he hasn't been to for several owners now, that's the last he hears of the incident on the Kelly plantation, which means that Sheriff Boudreaux has kept his mouth shut. Daniel suspected he would, and he's happy he saw his old friend. Over the next week, his routine of driving the ferry, working in the garage, and sleeping hard at night restores itself. Clive and Haley go about their business as if nothing has happened, taking their long drives in the evening, quietly screwing in the room down the short hallway from Daniel's. Some nights he half-wakes to hear them leaving when the front door whines, going for a late-night drive or a six-pack maybe, and against worry he gives himself to sleep's undertow. Each day, as he drives the motor ferry from one bank to the other, daydreams of a great flood wash him in a narcotic blandness that makes the time rush past him like a river of whiteness, and when he crawls into bed at night, he recalls nothing of his days.

He's finishing his morning coffee at the rail, watching the treacherous river currents roll over one another, when an usher stops beside him, wanting to tell someone about last night's fire at the Mimosa Groves plantation house in the next county. Having enjoyed this morning's hush, no radio or TV, Daniel wakes right up and listens to the whiskery guy. The sheriffs there left an empty cruiser at the end of the plantation's service road, faithful that its presence would deter any would-be arsonist. Around three they responded to a call about Mimosa Groves and found the 183-year-old house consumed in hot gasoline blaze. As before, the sheriffs suspect no one.

In town, after work, Daniel visits the video rental shop, the post office, a gas station, the library, renting and buying and borrowing for the sake of appearance, really just collecting information, and learns that his fellow townsfolk are all suspicious of one another. At the butcher's, his eyes on the stuffed pork chops on special, he waits in line behind two women comparing the alibis of their loved ones.

"My Chris was out, but he was at the Blue Moon with his friends. He said there were more than forty people who can account for it."

"He'd never think to do that anyhow. Now, the twins, they're young enough that I could see them cooking up something like that, just because they don't understand the seriousness of it all. You should hear them and their friends; they think it's cool. And they sneak out all the time, to go skateboarding with their friends at midnight. But they don't have a car, so they couldn't have gone out that far."

"Really? You think your boys would do something like that?"

"You wouldn't believe the things they used to do to the dog. Boys that age are cruel-minded."

"Ain't that the truth? But these arsons aren't anything they would get up to. These are the act of a through-and-through madman. They're about us, too. In our very midst."

Sensing an uncomfortable silence, Daniel looks up to see both women look quickly away from him. They flinch and then turn their backs to watch the butcher, in his bloody apron, carefully weigh two handfuls of ground sirloin on the counter scale. One of them mentions the new doctor's office going up on the edge of the town. The other says she's impressed by the fast work. They chatter as if Daniel has disappeared from behind them.

He waits, stiff with anger and the will to calm himself. He's been excluded like this since his childhood, and where normally his pride would heal him little fears gobble like piranha. Since hearing about Mimosa Groves he's tried to reconstruct the previous night, only to find himself stopped at the black wall of his sleep. He vividly remembers an incident from Clive's childhood, a little while after Daniel and Lucy married, when a sheriff brought the boy home because he and two other boys were caught trying to set fire to a kitten in the trees behind the baseball diamonds. The little cat, alive and well aside from a singed tail, belonged to another kid, one whom Clive's partners in crime said his stepson liked to bully at school. Fearing she'd raised a little pyromaniac, Lucy sent her son to a therapist, who after a few meetings with Clive assured her that a fascination with fire wasn't uncommon among children. He doubted that Clive was actually a firebug. Lucy was relieved by the man's opinion, and Daniel was unsurprised, having in his childhood known many boys who tortured animals at one time or another. Sure enough, the next time a sheriff brought Clive home, it was for shoplifting, and the time after that, it was for striking a younger boy in the head with bat. He and Lucy forgot all about the kitten with the burned tail.

The episode returns to him as he drives home to find the house empty, as he searches the armoire and the strewn-about clothes in Clive and Haley's bedroom for some scrap of evidence that his stepson is an arsonist. He remembers it as he gazes in on the contents of his refrigerator. He takes a cold beer and sits on the front step, still wearing his sweat-stained work clothes, and waits for Clive and Haley to appear. He plans to question Clive this time and tries to invent a justification for burning those houses, for keeping it a secret from the town. The sour beer helps him stretch out time, put off thinking.

He's alarmed when a sheriff's cruiser parks at the curb but breathes a little when he sees Boudreaux at the wheel, dressed in a T-shirt, waving at him. He stands as his old friend climbs out of the car and crosses the yard carrying a twelve-pack, shaking his head and wearing a puzzled smile. "You heard about the fire, right?"

"Yeah, who hasn't?" Daniel stares at the sheriff's tucked-in shirt and knee-high socks. He can't remember the last time he saw Boudreaux out of his beige uniform. The man's put on a few pounds since the days they hunted ducks together with the sheriff's dogs.

"I'd offer you a beer, but it seems our thoughts were in the same phase. This'll make a healthy surplus." Boudreaux unleashes a beast of a handshake, and they take a seat on the front step. Once the sheriff has enjoyed his first sip he holds his head aloft, as if in solemn thought. "That was the fifth house to go up. The forensics report came back and said that it was a gasoline fire, same as the others. But they're saying this is probably one of those copycat crimes."

"Why's that?"

"The fire was started on the ground floor. In the others, whoever did it started a separate fire on each one. Now we got a man watching the Kelly place every night, from ten until dawn. Clive still working there?"

"I doubt anyone else would hire him, so there's not a whole lot of choice. Clive only got the job because Kelly was in a rush to get down to his beach house. Guy hates him, talks to him like he's a child."

Boudreaux laughs at this. "Old man Kelly's not an easy man to get to like you. And I don't expect Clive helped him out in that area."

"The kid won't look at him." Saying this, Daniel swells with pride. He's always liked to see stuffy old money folks like Kelly annoyed by peasants like him. "But the job keeps Haley in plastic jewelry and milkshakes."

"The important things in life," Boudreaux says. "I used to think those were the law and the church. Then I got married." He peers back at the quiet house. "Where are the lovebirds?"

"Out driving. Maybe parked somewhere."

"Too bad I'm off duty."

They watch the homecoming traffic stream into the neighborhood, and as the expensive cars and their well-dressed drivers pass they speak of unimportant things, easing themselves back into the grooves of their old friendship. Grateful for the sheriff's gentle manner, Daniel is beset by a sweet aching with each smile and look into his old friend's eyes. He wishes he had held on to this friendship. Just this one. After Lucy died, he stopped talking to everyone. He didn't answer the telephone, ignored the doorbell, and when people turned back it was easy to blame them. How stupid he feels now, seeing his former self for a confused and bitter man, locking his door against help. Boudreaux asks for his thoughts on the weather, rescuing him from this self-torture. Daniel discovers he has theories of weather patterns on the coastal plain, from working so long on the river. Just as the sweeping rains make room for brilliant days, they turn to talk of the changing town, how the fountains have remained teeming with frogs for over forty years, of former classmates who've died, of canals and fields they once hunted, now too polluted or overrun by new generations of hunters to go back to.

"You remember when we stole the auto ferry?"

"Of course I remember stealing the auto ferry." They'd come puttering back to the dock, drunk and mortified by the machine and the river they'd taken on. The sheriffs had been waiting for them and kept them in the Wayne cell until dawn.

"You remember why we stole the auto ferry?" Boudreaux sniggers into his fist, his face sincerely confused and yet mocking puzzlement.

"We wanted to see if anybody would notice if we did it."

"Yeah, right on, and you knew how to drive it, even back then. You had a sixth sense," Boudreaux says. "You were made to drive that thing."

"Hell, they made you a sheriff."

"Justice is a mysterious thing."

They've finished most of the twelve-pack when Clive's red pickup pulls into the driveway, and he and Haley gaze a moment at the scene on the front porch. Clive says something and they both get out. He slowly comes around the front of the truck, squinting at Boudreaux, who drunkenly waves at him. Haley, less intimidated, walks smiling up the sidewalk, her purse dangling at her side. She stops in front of Daniel and the sheriff and flirtatiously cocks a hip to one side. The sheriff looks at her breasts long enough to study them. She grins. "Hey y'all. Looks like you two boys are up to no good."

Boudreaux jabs a finger at Daniel and says, "It's all his fault. He flagged me down and got me drunk as a goat."

"That true, Daniel?"

He shrugs, taken a little aback by the shift in the sheriff's demeanor, remembering now that Boudreaux has always put on a show for attractive women.

"Well, you ought to be ashamed, corrupting an officer of the law like that."

Daniel goes along with the joke, mimicking the sheriff's drunkenness, and holds out his fists side by side. "Better put the cuffs on me." The sheriff guffaws at this.

Haley widens her eyes and looks at the cruiser. "He driving home?"

"Somebody's got to," Boudreaux says, and his glad entirety trembles with laughter.

Clive steps up beside his girlfriend, flashing his teeth, watching the sheriff. He shifts his weight from foot to foot and holds up a hand in greeting.

"Hey, Clive, how you doing? Yard work treating you good?" Boudreaux winces back a burp. "You look fit."

"Yeah." Clive frowns. "Yeah, I'm getting into shape."

Daniel sees them all drift toward an awkward silence. He puts in, "You should have seen the anthill he stepped into the other day. Blisters all over his ankle."

"That right?" says Boudreaux. "Well, let's see it."

After looking from Daniel to the sheriff, Clive leans against Haley and pulls up his right pant leg, revealing a welter of broken red bites, the size of tennis ball.

The sheriff whistles. "Shooee, better put some Calamine on that, boy."

"I'm about to," he says, patting Haley lightly on the back. "Come on."

Boudreaux purses his lips, watching them go into the house. "Well, he's done something right. I tell you what, Daniel, I think he's going to be just fine." His voice goes rueful and he looks Daniel in the face. "You know, I remember we had some trouble, too. There was a time when things weren't looking so good for either of us."

"I know that," says Daniel.

"And we turned out just fine. Just fine. Look at us now." The sheriff laughs again, a high-pitched sound that grows plaintive. He frowns bitterly and glares out at the band of pink light thickening behind the houses of the street.

After he's gone home, promising to drive carefully, his words follow Daniel into the garage, where the parts of a weed-whacker lie in neat disassembly on the wooden work table. He goes around Lucy's old car to the table and stands not thinking, listening to the voices of his stepson and Haley on the other side of the door to the kitchen. Their words are unclear, but he listens only for the sounds of their voices, a warm river of syllables that swells up around him, raising him, carrying him to thoughts of Lucy.

He'd been trying to understand why he hated his town, why, when he tried to leave, he hated the flowering forests that climbed bluffs over low green rivers. Even miles out of the woods, where the fields of faintly yellow grass gave way to the pure cornflower blue spread over the gulf, he never felt as if he'd escaped. So he'd stayed but went mad in his parents' house, and one night found himself at the bathroom sink, poking himself in the neck with a razor. He didn't understand himself, or the sadness that sometimes rinsed over him when he went into town and couldn't find a single person he was happy to see. Then came the hospital, where he'd talked to doctors, stayed up all night reading Gurdjieff, and exercised each day, surrounded by men and women who'd lost the will to be themselves, who'd maybe never had that will in the first place.

It wasn't long before he felt ready to try again. He took the job on the ferry's driving platform, hoping that random opportunity would awaken a calling in him to be some kind, any kind of man. At first full of uncertainty about the tiresome work, the heat, and the grime, he was struck by the thought that his hopes had been answered when he saw Lucy Anderson climbing the iron stairs, holding the hem of her floral print dress in one hand as she stepped. As teenagers they'd noticed one another in school and around town, but she had married young and he'd given up dreaming of her. Shortly before he'd committed himself at the hospital, the news that her husband had been killed in a four-wheeler accident only depressed him, and he'd missed the funeral, not wanting to see her mourning. When he saw her climbing the steps to him, an older wiser Lucy, but one still certain of her interest in him, he opened up to wanting her, love and a woman, after years of learning to settle for disappointment. They'd been a happy pair, despite her grief, despite his coldness to her friends and people in town, despite her son's loss of control. It wasn't first love, but this was better, sharing what they had in a small house in the nothing historic neighborhood of a nothing town. Going back to the past, here in the garage, his happy past, he finds it worth living for, even if he's getting old and tired and spending too much time tinkering in his garage. Compelled to throw open the kitchen door and tell Haley and Clive to uncork a bottle of wine, he hovers with his hand at the doorknob, clearly hearing their words for the first time.

"Still, there's no way that sheriff knows," Clive's saying. He sounds uncertain and paces in the kitchen.

"Maybe," she says almost crying, "but that house is ready to go up. You better take care of it tonight. Just to be safe. And then that's the end of this shit. Clive, I mean it. I don't know how you get yourself into this shit. I don't know why I put up with it."

"Don't worry. I don't know how it started." Daniel senses them beyond the door, embracing in the center of the kitchen. "I don't know how it got hold of me but I can stop. I can stop."

"Maybe the sun could somehow start the fire. If you just let it alone."

Daniel lingers there in his dirty work clothes, all his knowledge swirling in the cloud of his discernment of what will happen and what can. He feels his hands moving at his sides, their action unintelligible to him, and when he looks down he's holding his copies of Clive's keys. Outside there is yet a little sunlight, time enough before the sheriffs move in on the Kelly house to take their positions. All his neighbors are in their houses, moving toward meals, toward loved ones, into glad voices and warm skin. He can see the entire town radiating out from his house, the grid of empty streets, him at the wheel of his dead wife's car, harnessing what he's learned about this town and its people, this house and its things, through haunting it. He knows his decision before he knows why. Because redemption is a reality with a son and daughter, because an empty house is worth less than one with people in it, because the past is made of wood and iron and stone, because he is flesh and blood, because there is time. He takes a box of wood matches from a drawer in the work table before he goes out into the twilight.

GHOST STORIES

As the story went, the Dravinski family lived on a federally owned wildlife preserve south of the city. The man of the house, a naturalist, had gone to high school with Erik's father, the sort of friend who never dropped in without a buddy. On the day this Dravinski telephoned, Erik saw his father happier than he had seen him since July ended and the ubiquitous reefs of dead, decaying mayflies joined the unremarkable past. There had been no great loss to speak of, but it had been one of those quiet periods during which the house felt unmistakably sad to Erik, when he and his parents all seemed separated by an insurmountable gulf. Now, squinting in shady amusement, his father hollered into the telephone, howled laughter, and spoke in clipped sentences. He called up a litany of strange last names — Kovacs, Horvath, Materni, Farkas — happily remembering the humiliations of high school. He faced into a corner, as if his wife and son couldn't possibly fathom his giddiness.

They would get their chance. The Dravinskis were throwing a party that weekend. His father couldn't understand why his wife shrugged and retreated to the living room, where she could read a mystery in peace, or why Erik sighed in defeat and slunk out into the yard, dreading the introduction to still more people who were probably cooler than he. "You don't *live* in a wildlife preserve," Erik said to himself, going out to the vegetable garden, jar in hand, to hunt moles. His mother liked to kill them, so he relocated them to the field. "You *dwell* in a wildlife preserve."

It was a long drive down the road that passed the point where the Maumee River widened to rapids. It was a Saturday in late

September, an evening the color of honey, mosquitoes cruising. Inside, the car smelled of vinyl cleaner and his mother's perfume, last of all the wind. They drove past corn fields and a graveyard on a high hill, as well as several barns converted to cider stores with gaudy, hand-painted signs and displays of tomatoes and blackberries set out front. This world of frank beauty was near Toledo, but you'd have never guessed it, and if its residents wanted to keep it a secret to preserve it, Erik sympathized. He was thirteen years old, short and soft-bellied, humiliated in all ways by the absence of puberty signs, except for his voice, which had always been deep. Though they lived in the suburbs, he went to a Catholic school on the east side with boys whose parents worked in factories and restaurants. At recess in the school parking lot, they liked to wait for him to approach them, accuse him in loud voices of releasing an egregious fart, then flee across the blacktop. School days were long and tedious and scarred with his humiliations, but the solitude of the weekends was harder on him.

As they traveled along, he tried to care about the local lore his father remembered. A man who drove a DeLorean lived in these hills. He zipped down the highway on Sunday afternoons, while the sheriffs ate biscuits and gravy in Grand Rapids. Erik thought cars were boring and dirty, and he was a little afraid of men who were enthusiastic about them. They drove past a seasonal carnival, its red and orange lights dull, its small Ferris wheel and roller coaster buried in a patch of woods. His father claimed to have taken him there before he was old enough to walk. What a waste that seemed, but his parents smiled at the memory. They passed a former boys' reformatory, Catholic, like so many of the region's institutions from the early part of the century. A tall, brick, vaguely military edifice on a hill near the river. His father said it was haunted by the ghosts of abused boys, all of them around Erik's age.

"Peter, let's not go into the Twilight Zone," said Erik's mother. She had her window down, and her wispy hair, dyed red, flickered over the headrest of the ultramarine seat.

"I'm just trying to cultivate a healthy fear of boarded-up buildings in the child," said Erik's father. He was a famous joker. His wife and son knew better. "Who knows what a little hooligan he'll turn out to be?" He laughed, a vigorous *ha ha ha*, with eyes comically large in the rearview mirror.

"Honey," said Erik's mother, "you're not at the party yet."

Erik was curious about the reformatory that now lay beyond the weeping willows getting smaller behind them. He could still see Spanish roof and clerestory windows. He had glimpsed, as they passed the proud structure, the stony dome of a grotto behind it. How many sulking boys had gone there, assumed the position of prayer, and then escaped into the rich shadows of the mind? He closed his eyes and saw a mess hall with high, curtained windows, corridors of miserable little sleeping quarters, bathrooms full of boys in white nightshirts. They spoke only in these moments of privacy. Here they traded cigarettes and playing cards with crude drawings of female nudes. A boy was humiliated, dragged into a stall. Priests roamed the halls with paddles and righteous frowns. Erik would have liked to have been one of the incarcerated, to have had a friend and a window on the third floor, to have broken out one foggy night. They would have lighted out up the river, toward the forests of Michigan, resilient as Huck Finn but never so lighthearted. That was the life Erik wanted, to be always on the run. You couldn't trust people, and the ones you could trust bored you.

The Dravinski house was a long ranch built off the preserve's main road, beside a giant ponderosa pine. A wooden patio extended from the back of the house and let down stairs on a broad yard framed by tall pine trees. There was a trampoline bouncing children into the air near a soccer field where older boys ran, shouting. Their shoes fascinated Erik. Strange brands, clearly expensive. Because his parents were impressed enough to discuss it between themselves, Erik knew that the older Dravinski boys attended St. John's, one of the best Catholic high schools in the city. From the sports page he knew such schools had soccer teams. St. Boniface did not offer its young students the option to play soccer. How privileged that seemed, a world in which looks were taken care of for you, and you only had to choose a sport to play. The boys all had fabulous haircuts, long on top and parted in the middle, the sides and back of the head shaved. How these hairdos flopped about, like bushes in a storm, as their wearers chased the fickle ball.

Adults crowded near the garage, drinking keg beer, holding paper plates. Dogs chased each other in the yard, entertainment for some, who pointed and remarked. A three-acre lawn of even, healthy grass. Erik recalled a newspaper story about deer ticks, and the skin of his legs swarmed with thousands of phantom legs.

They parked among the cars along the road, with a view of the far side of the house. There was a volleyball pit, older girls, a few kids about Erik's age, a spike by a tall girl. One boy had removed his shirt, and his torso flashed, reddish in the dusk, to strike back the descending ball. These kids would determine Erik's career at the party, and he was beginning to sweat as his heartbeat quickened. Usually, larger boys picked on him, and girls found him an oddity, but he hung on the edge of their groups because there was only one party that meant anything. Isolation afforded him fantasies, but he had the rest of his life to pretend.

His father's one requirement was that he meet the Dravinskis. Gerald was tapping a fresh keg, handsomer and fitter than his former schoolmate. Erik's father lowered his head a little, oddly shy. He was slow to look either Dravinski in the face. Donna

Dravinski wore khaki shorts and a pink sleeveless blouse, blonde hair to her shoulders. She was prettier than Erik's mother. Beyond looks, Erik saw their bodies were different from his parents'. The Dravinskis were younger somehow. Their faces shone with the unchallenged optimism of the healthy. Erik foresaw a discussion of this on the drive home. His parents would agree that life on a wildlife preserve was better for the skin and the waistline, then travel on in silence. He held out his hand reluctantly to each of the Dravinskis, and when he'd muttered answers to their lame questions about school, he set out for the volleyball pit on the far side of the house.

The challenge mounting before him was to catch the interest of the kids his age. He lacked the good looks, flair, athleticism, and nice clothes that other boys relied on to admit them through the passageways to teenage popularity. When he had transferred to St. Boniface, he had hoped to simply blend into the popular group like a chameleon and to be one day discovered, to the joy of his peers, as their beloved friend, an inseparable part of their crowd. Where would we be without Erik? they'd ask each other — a rhetorical question because the answer was obviously nowhere. Perhaps it had been his strategic lingering at the edge of their recess discussion, distracted by this vision, that had led to the class hyena's spontaneous invention that he emitted toxic gases, and the boys' subsequent, cackling flight.

Now he was careful not to get too close to the volleyball game, lest one of the players turn out to be another ruthless comedian. He took a place beneath the long curved branches of the ponderosa in the front yard and was grateful to find there an immense pine cone. He inspected it with real interest, though also to look like the scientific type, his presence incidental. The pine cone was the size of a softball, and as he turned it in both hands, admiring its thick scales, a tiny spider leapt onto his wrist. He cried out and dropped the pine cone. He slapped himself as the spider jumped into the grass.

He heard laughter and felt the attention of the kids in the volleyball pit. An older girl called out to him. Was he okay?

Erik gave a grim nod. The shirtless boy began to argue with a boy on the other side of the net, saying that this last point did not count because this new kid had screamed and scared everyone and that was no way to end the fifth game in a tied series. The others in the pit joined the argument, and the far side's team began to brag that it had won the match. To solidify their victory they dispersed in the direction of the party, talking of desserts.

Feeling a strong urge to apologize, Erik approached the near side's team. A tall girl with long blonde hair had picked up her sandals from beside the net. She explained to the shirtless boy that she was tired of playing anyway. She smiled at Erik, but the gesture was marked by pity. She was sixteen or older anyhow, so he was no candidate for her romance. He held the tight dimples of his false smile. The other team members were walking away. He found himself facing the shirtless boy, alone.

"Sorry about that," he said.

"Forget it," said the boy, looking after his teammates. "As far as I'm concerned, they all just forfeited. Nobody comes to the Dravinski home court and wins. Not that easy."

Erik nodded, estimating this boy's intelligence to be about average. Hope radiated from his mouth and eyes, he knew. He put his hands in the pockets of his bargain basement shorts in an approximation of nonchalance. He had befriended a kind of athlete before, purely physical boys who only cared for constant movement, which they felt all the more without their shirts. After a time they always recognized their mistake and fled him. But it was already late, and they might not reach that point. Maybe this kid would even invite Erik to hang out in his room, to show off his trendy possessions. He looked like the kind of boy you wanted to leave with a high opinion of you. He already had blonde hair in his armpits and a braid of muscles in his stomach. He had the same wonderful bowl haircut the older boys sported. Erik could tell he had girlfriends by his ease in talking to the older girl. He smelled of bug repellant and regarded Erik with small blue eyes.

"What were you screaming about?" he asked.

"I wouldn't call it a scream," said Erik. "A spider jumped out of the pine cone."

"There are worse things than spiders out here," said the boy. "Maybe you should go in the house and watch TV. It's safer in there."

"It's no big deal," said Erik. "I just wasn't prepared for it. The same spiders live in my yard at home. The little jumping ones, with striped bodies. You know, the ones that crouch."

"I hate those little bastards," the boy told him. "I'm Brad."

The sun had fallen behind the trees, and the long yard was a trough of shadows. Brad announced he was going to get a Manwich, which sounded made-up, cannibalistic, and faintly homosexual. Erik felt cautious and curious, as if he'd received a key to a witch's tower, but Brad made no protest when he went along. In the garage was a table covered with a paper cloth. Adults stood around, happy and drinking, their faces marvelous masks in the light of three ceiling bulbs. A Manwich, it turned out, was a sloppy joe. Orangeish meat steamed in a crock pot. There were bubbles. Erik made a small sandwich that he didn't want, while Brad covered a paper plate with potato salad and baked beans. Sodas lay iced in a red cooler at the end of the table. They sat on an old railroad tie that had been used to terrace the garden around the garage, Brad ravenous, Erik holding the forgotten sandwich. Two floodlights had been switched on to illuminate the soccer field, and the game of the older boys continued.

Brad began to talk about a new episode of a show called *Seinfeld*. He said his favorite parts of the program were the segments of stand-up comedy. He ate his Manwich and talked confidently, like a sports fan at a game.

Erik had never heard of *Seinfeld*. His parents watched *Sixty Minutes*, *The McLaughlin Group*, and *Fawlty Towers*. He was rarely allowed to watch television. His mother brought him vhs releases by Fairy Tale Theater from the public library. These he enjoyed in shameful privacy, drifting further and further, he knew, from the norm. He listened closely to Brad's banter, ready to laugh at the precise moment the other boy did.

"I think that in the future there will be TV shows that are all stand-up," said Brad. "That's one thing to look for in television. My dad even says so. It's on the way."

"You're probably right," said Erik. He thought of the boys' reformatory they had passed on the way and wanted to tell Brad about the grotto, but he restrained himself. He had identified his desire to mention Huck Finn. If there was anything that other boys hated, it was when he began to talk about characters in books. He had made this mistake at St. Boniface once, mentioning Taran Pig-Boy, only to hear, in response, the shout, "Erik farted!" and the cries of mock-horror that accompanied it.

"Have you seen the new *Nightmare on Elm Street*?" asked Brad.

"No," said Erik, afraid he might let out an involuntary sob. It was on the back of his tongue, pacing, throwing up its hands in frustration. He worried that Brad would stand up and leave him, this boring imposter at his parents' party. He had to keep talking, to keep Brad's attention until his words brought him to something cool to say. "No, but we passed a haunted reformatory on the way here. There's a shrine behind it made of rocks."

Brad sighed through his nose and watched the soccer game.

"It's true," said Erik. "We stopped, because my dad studies

ghosts. He's a phantomologist." This was not true. His father sat in a bank all week, thinking about and moving other people's money. Erik went on, trusting himself, against his better judgment. "He wanted my mom and me to see it. But the building was locked, with a big No Trespassing sign hanging on it. It's been locked up for years because the sightings have caused several people to lose their minds. Now they're homeless people. There are messages written in blood on the bathroom mirrors. I especially wanted to see those. But we just listened at the door. Something scratched the other side."

"I bet it was a raccoon," said Brad.

"That's what I told my dad," said Erik, sure to make eye contact. "So he took us around back to the shrine. We had to step down into it, and the air was wet, like in a basement. There was a statue of Mary there and a place to kneel. So we all got down there and knelt and closed our eyes. We held our hands like we were praying but we didn't pray. And then we heard it."

"What?" Brad folded his messy paper plate and crumpled it in his hands.

"We heard crying. All around us. The sound of boys wailing in pain. My dad thought they were the voices of kids who went down there to pray." He held his eyes wide open, afraid to look unafraid of ghosts.

Brad looked around at the faces of the preoccupied adults. He whispered, "Show me."

"It's too far," said Erik, relieved, close to sealing the fib. "It's a half hour by car."

"My brother will take us," said Brad. He looked toward the soccer game, unsure. Then he shook his head. A moth fluttered past. He turned to face the woods. "We have ghosts out here, too," he said. "You want to see?"

"Yes," said Erik. The thought of the woods, full of discomforts, made him cold all over. The trees here were taller than those near his house in the suburbs, and he had noticed, when it was still light, dense ground-level brush. He expected vines, poison ivy, thorny bushes. But here was the golden offer of friendship, the invitation to the secret on the grounds. He had a sense that the night could go on, defy the turning motion of the earth, and never end. Erik knew with a fierce certainty that he must sustain this feeling. "Yes," he said. "Let's go."

He followed Brad through the house, surprised by the black iron stove and the mounted heads of elk on the log walls. The lustrous wooden floors were covered in throw rugs, soft under Erik's feet. They had removed their shoes at the door. No one did this at Erik's house, and as a result the carpets were stained and tough in places. The kitchen shone with new appliances. By comparison to the Dravinskis, Erik's family lived in a dust trap, a storage closet for stacks of financial papers. All the rooms of their house had a quality of attics, of stillness interrupted by sudden light.

Brad opened a closet and climbed past the coats inside. He came out with two large flashlights. He held them like Indian clubs, reconsidered Erik as if he might not be trustworthy to handle the family's things, then conceded and handed one over.

"It's heavy," said Erik, hefting the thing like he would a short baseball bat.

"These are what the cops in L.A. beat the gang-bangers with," said Brad. He held his at arm's length and turned it over. Erik presumed this was all very impressive, and said, "Wow."

"Yeah buddy."

They sneaked out the side door. A light came on above the porch, and they saw an older boy and girl who were standing close, touching, on the sand of the volleyball pit, look up and step away from each other. The boy scratched in his cool bowl haircut and frowned at his foreign shoes.

Brad stood with his feet apart, his mouth slightly open. He breathed once and said, "Get off of my property."

Anger surfaced in the older boy's eyes. It quickly sank again, and he relaxed his shoulders and looked away. The girl, her arms crossed defensively, stared at them like a child caught stealing. Erik instantly pitied her. He would remember her fondly. He would wish to have been her friend, then more.

Brad said, "Get out of here, or I'm going to tell Cal."

The girl said, "Brad, please don't."

The older boy rolled his eyes, produced a battered baseball cap from his back pocket, and started for the cars parked along the road. "I'm going," he said. The girl looked at him with gorgeous concern, started to follow, then turned quickly on Brad.

"Please don't say anything to your brother," she said.

Erik watched her catch up with the older boy. He should have been that guy, he thought, the one with the thick chest and the chin stubble. Where were they going? The air had turned dangerous, full of unpredictable movement. A cool breeze lay on his arms. Brad was walking away toward a fortress of trees. Erik ran to catch him, tight in the chest, desperate for knowledge and camaraderie. The quest for ghosts was spoiled now, a child's pastime. The trek through woods loomed ahead like a terrible chore. He knew to keep his voice low.

He caught up with Brad. "Who was that?"

"My brother's old girlfriend," said Brad. "When I tell Cal, he's going to kick that guy's ass."

"Shouldn't you tell him now?" Erik asked. He hoped to see a shouting match, a fistfight, the girl crying. He wanted to comfort her.

Brad turned to the road. The couple had driven off in a dark sedan. "Cal will whip him later," he said. His self-assurance calmed him. He faced Erik in the darkness. "Come on, we'll go in right up here."

They reached the edge of the woods and stopped. Erik's eyes adjusted. Low branches and underbrush reached like arms around a low opening in the trees. He expected to fall down right away, but he was unwilling to return to the party by himself. He watched as Brad ducked and pushed through the branches.

"It's not bad once you get inside. We can't turn the flashlights on until we're farther in."

Erik believed him until he had taken a few steps into the darkness. His shoes caught in brambles, his ankles were immediately scratched. Above him he saw the dense weave of a thicket against the broad fans of pine limbs. The footsteps in front of him were getting away, leaving him in this snare. He prayed for an abrupt opening, the discovery of an easy passage, and pursued Brad. There was a narrow, trampled path, its edges thorned and ferny. He walked fast, bent over, until a flashlight switched on just ahead and blinded him. Gradually Brad appeared, illuminated, solemn, as if he were about to tell a ghost story. Erik found he could stand. Above lay a crude maze of night sky, stars. Crickets nearby grew silent.

"Come on," said Brad. "This path goes to the old cabin."

They walked on quickly, light with anticipation. An owl called from somewhere, in brief bewilderment. Mosquitoes found them and attacked. They were relentless. Erik swatted them and wiped the blood from his arms, calves, and face.

Brad talked about his brother's ex-girlfriend. "They might still get back together. That's why Cal invited her. I don't know what that kid was thinking. Cal is going to kick his ass. If he doesn't, Greg will." Greg was the oldest brother, Erik remembered from his parents' conversation, a senior at St. John's. He would apply to Ivy League schools this fall, they had said. He wished his parents weren't so impressed by the Dravinskis, because he was, too. He didn't understand why his parents didn't change their lives. The owl hooted again and was cut off by Brad saying, "That's one thing the Dravinskis can't have, guys messing with their women."

The path narrowed and disappeared into a cluster of thick hawthorn bushes. Their round berries turned red to black as Erik flashed his beam over them. He saw the long thorns, the branches like cords, and hesitated. He feared for his eyes and saw himself emerging from the woods flailing, his skin laced with scratches. He remembered that Brad lived here and thought he must know a way around this obstacle. "Where to now?"

Brad stood, rethinking their predicament. He looked helpless, still shirtless, his arms folded, like a young faun still learning about the forest. His mouth was wider than his eyes. He held his light on the gray-green leaves. "These weren't here before," he said. He pressed his lips small and colorless, and glowered. It was as if he was tormented by the thought that they had been growing here all along. He shrugged and said, "We'll have to just go through them."

Erik was about to protest when Brad plunged into them, shouting in pain and surprise. The flashlight revealed only thrashing shrubbery and the unconscious swaying of upper branches. Brad's cries became steadier, louder, more determined. The bush continued to thrash. This seemed like the right time to turn back, Erik decided. Not to see the cabin would be a disappointment, but he preferred the cozy backseat of his father's car to going any further. He waited for Brad to reappear, bleeding and vanquished. He heard zany laughter.

"I'm here!" Brad shouted from the far side of the bush. "Rad! Come on, man! Do it!"

With great reluctance Erik faced a cruel fact about this universe, how never getting to a place prevented you from knowing whether it was, finally, just as you'd imagined it. Brad knew this, too, which was why they had come out here. He closed his eyes, crossed his hands before his face, and charged into the brush. Long thorns lodged in his arms and tore his clothes. It was as if he had fallen into a carpenter's laundry. All over his body the points of intolerable pain were too many to count, and his desire to go back drowned in his fear that he was closer to the other side. He growled and squealed and fought through the bushes until, gurgling, he stumbled out, nearly running into Brad.

The other boy wore the smile of an idiot who promotes leaping out of airplanes. He gestured at a small log cabin sitting atop a knoll covered in high grass. "Here we are," said Brad. "Ghost central."

The brutal feeling vanished as Erik shone his light over the dark windows. Fallen leaves and branches covered the roof. Patches of wood showed where shingles had fallen away. It was the perfect clubhouse, a place to live apart from your lunatic family, close enough so you could still go home for rations. He would have moved his stuff out here years ago.

"Let's go in," he said. He started through the grass, leaving Brad behind him. At the windows he held his flashlight against the warped glass. His elbows cooled on the stone ledge. Inside, a wooden table stood bare beside a short, stout icebox. In one corner a thin mattress lay on a rusty bed frame. It was a perfect villain's hideout. He could see himself, living here, sitting at the table, keeping a journal of animal sightings. Occasionally he would be visited by other outlaws who needed his advice. None of them would have been so well established as to have a cabin, and they would naturally look up to him. The police would come and question him, and he would shrug off their questions, let the rustic accoutrements of his simple existence do the talking. He felt Brad standing behind him. "I bet criminals stay here all the time. Ever see any?"

"What?" Brad stood quietly, his flashlight pointed into the long grass that reached past the cuffs of his khaki cut-offs. He seemed to be thinking. "Um," he said. "Once my dad found a family of raccoons inside."

"Let's go in," said Erik. He was struck by the possibility that the ghost of a pioneer inhabited this structure, that if he lived here he could lie in bed at night and watch canned goods float around the room. The ghost of the pioneer would write in his own journal, nostalgic for the days when Indians visited the cabin, instead of common lawbreakers.

"We can't go in," said Brad. "It's locked. The ghosts are out here. My brothers both saw them. Look out."

Erik stared at this shadowed boy in disbelief. He saw how a little brother could be the composite copy of older ones. There Brad was, trapped by the lies he could not make work in his own words. Without his circle of young adults, he was barely more than animal. Erik would have said all this if he'd thought that it would do any good, but he suspected Brad had never been disobedient in a way his brothers had not. The owl called again.

"Did you hear that?" said Brad.

"That was an owl," said Erik.

"How do you know?" Brad sounded annoyed. "Can you see it? Point it out. Prove it's not a ghost."

Erik walked around to the cabin door and felt gravel beneath his shoes. He turned and shone the light toward what appeared to be a lawn with large maples spaced out by a landscaper. Saplings grew up all around them. "Where does this path go?" he asked.

"Don't change the subject," said Brad. "It goes to the street. Where do you think it goes?"

"No, seriously," he said. "I just heard something. There was someone here."

"No there wasn't," Brad said. "Shut up. Did you really hear someone?"

"Listen, you can hear his footsteps." Erik shone his light over the high grass and young trees, then swung the beam across the trunk of a large ash tree. "There he is," he whispered.

Brad came up beside him, heat and the smell of deodorant rolling off his torso, breathing softly through his mouth. "Who is it?"

"It might be that guy from the party," Erik whispered. "The one with your brother's girlfriend. Maybe she's out here, too."

"No way. My brothers will kick his ass." Brad went forward into the yard, shining his own light around, over grass and bushes, trees and sky. He jerked to face one way and then the other, as if he expected whatever presence awaited him in the darkness to attack. "Come out, whoever you are," he called. "We're not afraid; there's a whole bunch of guys real close who are going to kick your ass."

Erik turned off his light and padded up the gravel, concentrating on Brad's back, the muscles knotting each time the boy shouted. He seemed so intent on watching the air in front of him that he had lost all sense of what lay behind him. Erik stood with his dark hands raised, feeling like a magician, and when he could no longer contain the giggling sensation deep in his stomach he leapt forward and grabbed Brad's bare shoulders.

Brad screamed, dropped his flashlight in the gravel, and began to thrash. The sound only lasted a moment, but the experience electrified Erik, for it was not a cry or a shout or a girlish shriek, but demonic, belonging in another world. He immediately let go of Brad's shoulders and jumped back, terrified and numb in the chest, unsure of whether to burst into laughter or run for the cover of adults.

Brad flailed his arms, scrubbing imaginary hands from his skin, and turned, gasping for breath, staring through the darkness at Erik. He made his hands into fists and punched Erik in both shoulders at once, pushing him back. "Motherfucker," he barked. "Give me my flashlight! I'm going to kill you! Give me my flashlight!'

Erik stood dazed as the boy snatched the flashlight from his hand, picked up the other from the grass, and took off in a dead sprint up the gravel path in the direction of what he had already said was the road. He plunged into the darkness of the trees and, a moment later, his voice echoing from the road, shouted, "Let's see you get back by yourself, asshole!" Then came the sound of his rubber soles pounding the pavement, and a moment later he was gone.

The sound of crickets closed in as Erik considered the boy's challenge and shrugged it off, accepted that it was as stupid as it sounded. There was only one road through this park, his father had told him, and he had only to follow it back. He did not move just yet. He felt friendly with the night. He thought of Brad's scream again and imagined him now, racing back to his house, too embarrassed and ashamed to see that he would soon decide against telling anyone what had happened out here, and then, gradually, so afraid of being alone in the dark that he wanted nothing more than to be back in the safety of his brightly lighted house. Slowly, and with more regret than he had ever expected, Erik began to laugh.

His mother drove home. His father had drunk too much beer. Wide awake, Erik sat in the back. The scratches on his shins hurt him the most, but he could nearly forget them in his search for the landmarks they had passed on the way here. The night had put them away. In the morning they would be set out for him to examine.

His father reminisced about high school and compared the party to the last reunion. "So Gerald and Donna got married and went into hiding in the woods. Weirdos."

His mother had rolled down her window to help her ignore the monologue. Erik smiled to himself, cocking an ear to listen to his father.

"You know, Erik," he said, "at one time I was engaged to Donna Dravinski, back when she was Donna Kelley. Way before I met your mother." Erik thought he saw his mother smile. "Yeah, I dumped her. Dumb hippie. Then she started seeing Gerald, and they both avoided me. It was like we weren't adults. They used to leave parties when I arrived." He chortled.

Erik's mother frowned. Erik leaned over the seat between his parents. His father turned to him, grinning, his breath full of beer. Large and jovial, he was a mad king, soaked in his happiness. Laughter bubbled up steadily from him. "Yeah, old Gerald, scared I was going to steal his woman! Scared everyone would! He moved to the woods. For safety!"

"Peter," said Erik's mother. "Come on." Fighting back laughter, she frowned.

In the morning they would be themselves. Erik received the promise of Monday's light, which missed the other side of the world. The pitted road swept beneath the car with its billion unimportant details. They were going home, where he still slept with the windows open. Each night, he listened for the first bird to wake up lost and call out to others, to let them know it was there, and to hear them call back.

VARIATIONS ON A THEME

✧

When the park service truck pulled up, I was in the bathhouse office, penciling water temperatures in the logbook. The hum of the running engine gave me a nauseated kind of relief. Ranger Chuck jogged in, kid face showing through red beard, soda bottle full of dip spit in hand. "You heard, right?" he said, meaning the radio traffic about the drowning in Volusia County.

The question made me flinch, though all day I'd kept the radio to my ear, hanging on each fuzzy word, while gray waves tossed fetid black seaweed onto the deserted beach. This guy must have been drunk, ignored repeated warnings, and wound up tangled and dead in the surf. The townies up north were blaming him, which probably seemed fair to about everyone but the bereaved.

"I was thinking we could go up there and get a peek at the body." Chuck looked at the bathhouse's collapsed sofa and the tide chart on the wall, growing uncertain as he translated his plan into words. "I've never even seen a body."

He tapped fingers on the thighs of his khaki pants like a boy anticipating something sweet. I tried not to be offended. He didn't know what happened with Elise back in Colorado. I hadn't told anyone in Cape Canaveral. Limiting my response to a frown, I shut the logbook and considered the tobacco shreds stuck in his yellow teeth.

Okay, I thought. Let's get you a peek.

The drive was thirty miles through the mosquito-infested palm forest and then across the causeway to a coastal plain disappearing under beach houses and commercial sprawl. Preferring the one-night-stand towns south of the monument, I never went up there, and so I ignored the dead armadillos on the road and the bugs collecting on the windshield and watched the shifting, iron-colored ocean go in and out of sight between the grassy dunes. Chuck sang along with Kenny Rogers and looked over at me from time to time.

The public wasn't allowed past the morgue's reception area, but Chuck knew the secretary, a plump, pretty young woman who burst into laughter when she saw him in his officer's uniform. It must have been the way she remembered him from high school, because he wasn't so much funny looking as young. By the way he toed the linoleum floor, I gathered people knew he was the kind of cop who confiscated tourist marijuana to smoke with the women he met at my bathhouse after hours.

"Don't let the gun and badge trick you," she said, toying with her large diamond engagement ring. "He's the biggest criminal out here."

"She thinks you're worthy of a superlative," I said.

Chuck shrugged. "Best reason to be a cop is you can break rules."

He grew solemn under the fluorescent lights, looking down on the clay-colored naked body of a young man. The blue eyes were open and staring, the pupils oblong and different sizes. There should have been some rule against leaving them open, and I would have shut them myself, but when I glanced up, the coroner's assistant, who begrudgingly tolerated our presence, was watching.

"It isn't what I expected," Chuck said. "I wish I could have done something."

He'd told me many times not to count on his help during a rescue. He never touched the sea, fearing jellyfish and sharks and all the other things it hid from you, though maybe he would have turned heroic in a time of need. I guess you never know what you can do until you're tested.

It was sad, seeing the dead guy. His swollen face was nicked up from the ocean floor, and he couldn't have been older than twenty-five. When Elise's car went down the ravine, her face was one thing that was spared in all the wreckage. For some shallow reason I had been comforted by this news, until I saw her and hardly recognized her with the facial muscles gone slack. She looked like some stranger wearing Elise's face.

I didn't know this guy before he died, though I was still sorry for him. You can't help but imagine what the person must have been like. The attendant was watching, but I placed quarters over his eyes anyway. Fuck it, I thought. Throw me out.

Chuck approved with a nod and long, sentimental sniff.

That night I met a woman in a dance club on the beach. I'd come home to see the night get down to business in the park. Cicadas and darkness owned the palm forest. White-bellied lizards crossed my windows, hunting palmetto bugs and mosquitoes. It was one of those occasions I found myself suspecting that I shouldn't have sold my car when I moved here. Down in Cocoa Beach, people were drinking in the clubs under the glowing walls of Ron Jon's Surf Shop, getting naked on the dark beaches. Feeling great pressure to join in, I called a taxi.

Inside the crowded bar, anxious to pay my cover and get alcohol in my bloodstream, I noticed a college-type girl in a green cotton dress standing by a row of stacked tables in the rear of the place. From across the room she looked so much like Elise that I knew I'd have to examine her for differences. Contrary to my expectations, the likeness increased the longer I looked. She had a chronic smiler's monkey cheeks, the short black hair and keen eyes, the same ripe little body. I felt a number of contradicting emotions and knew it would be best to walk out and find another place to drink. At the same time, I'd been around long enough to know I'd regret never learning just how much like Elise she was. This look-alike was drinking something red, and by the noncommittal way she sipped and stood with her arms crossed and her head cocked, not quite watching the people on the dance floor, I gathered she was alone.

The resemblance was stunning—in appearance they were almost the same. This girl was a little thinner, with an unhealthy gauntness in her cheeks, as if my fiancée hadn't eaten during her stay in the underworld. She narrowed her eyes as she watched me stare. Later she would say she was amused by the way I stood close and gawked, a tall man with grown-out blonde hair and a blue Hawaiian shirt, who had forgotten his own very conspicuous presence. She should have been alarmed. The city was filled with addicts and creeps and rapists, and so long as they had money, the good guys and bad guys all wore the same uniform. But the sense of familiarity between us erased all difficulty and concern. She put her drink's tiny red stirring straw to her lips and took a long sip. She smiled ironically and offered to shake my hand.

"I'm Janine."

"Okay," I said, studying the lines in her neck, ignoring the hand. When she widened her eyes and laughed, it dawned on me how foolish I appeared. Her laughter was sharper, more cynical than Elise's. My fiancée's character had been entirely earnest and kind. The wry gaze of this young woman was reminder enough of their separateness. I smiled and shook her hand just as she was about to revoke the offer.

I got us drinks and she invited me to sit on her side of the booth. She was just twenty. From my perspective, a ten-year difference wasn't much, but she knew better. She kept pinching my arm and poking me through my shirt, calling me dirty.

"Do you always hit on younger girls?"

I'd forgotten how young Elise had looked. "Well, the bar is for adults."

She shrugged. "Soon I'll be twenty-two and have to graduate and be serious."

I cringed thinking what a pain in the ass I'd been at that age.

Two hours later we were sitting on the beach, alternating between talking and making out with medium intensity, part of the restraint arising from my sense of unreality. Meeting women had never been a great challenge, but this had taken almost no effort at all, as if Janine had come to the bar expecting to meet someone and, finding me before her, accepted fate's offering without question. In fact, she was concerned with this very subject, using the little breaks from smooching to inquire about my zodiac sign and whether I knew anything about a fortune-teller who had told her to stop by after the bars closed.

"I have never heard of Madame Tammy," I confessed. "However, not knowing her doesn't prevent me from knowing it's probably a bad idea to go over there at night."

"I'd expect nothing less from a Leo," she said, looking up at the dense cloud mass hiding the stars. "You fire signs always want to take control."

"I am what I am."

"You're funny."

"I am what I am," I repeated. It was an old phrase of Elise's, an extremely funny and sexy thing when spoken by a forthright young lady who wants you naked immediately. I thought that if I said it enough around Janine she might start saying it. Imagining this gave me a sick, impish glee.

After a while the bars emptied and the beach filled with the shapes of people seeking privacy and others who wanted to observe them. Janine and I both wanted to be alone, so she led me to where she'd parked.

During my time in Florida I rode shotgun in many a single woman's vacuumed front seat. I loved the smell of bachelorettes' cars, how by singing a woman driver revealed the sexiness of her girly music, how she smiled to carry off her find, how she might suddenly grab my hand or lean over at an intersection to start kissing. No other came close to exciting me like Janine did, and not only because she looked like Elise. Whenever it occurred to me how much fun I was having, she'd shoot me a mischievous look, as if she'd heard me thinking.

After trolling many a dark street, we ended up after-drunk in a neighborhood of bungalows on an indigent stretch of the beach. Wide-awake residents sat up in plastic chairs on their sunken lawns, pinching their mentholated cigarettes and watching. A starved-looking man in ratty jean cutoffs trotted a beach cruiser past my window. My fear of these people made me vigilant like a snorkeler who has swum up on a barracuda, but Janine showed no fear. She was searching the mailboxes for the fortune-teller's address.

"I hope you know where you're going," I said, as we passed the Dead End sign. "We might have to back out of here pretty fast."

"Hush now." She looked for numbers on the dark little houses, which appeared tilted by the weight of the air conditioners in their windows. Cigarettes flared. Under her dress, I noticed, Janine wore a bikini spangled with stars. She leaned forward, and her nipples pressed through the thin material of the cups. I suddenly felt sure someone was in the backseat.

Seeing it was empty, I felt mildly disappointed.

"Don't worry so much," she said.

"I am what I am," I said quietly.

"There she is." In the road there stooped a bony, visibly drunk old woman in apparently nothing but an extra-large Bud Light T-shirt that hung to her knees. Beneath a mess of springy pink hair her eyes were half-closed. She beckoned for us to follow.

Janine and I held hands all the way to the rotten welcome mat. A shark's jawbone hung on the door like a knocker, and inside the house was decorated as if gypsies had come to town years earlier and remodeled the place for her. Tapestries embroidered with mandalas were tacked to the walls. Beside the oil lamp burning on a small wooden table, near a dirty ashtray and the remains of a microwave dinner, lay a deck of Tarot cards.

Madame Tammy placed a medallion on her forehead and brought us cans of beer, saying in her deep, harsh voice, "Get yourselves a seat."

Janine sat on the metal folding chair opposite the fortune-teller's place. She pressed her hands between her knees in anticipation. "So, Dennis." She sank her teeth into my name, the way Elise had. "What do you think the future has in store for me?"

I put a hand over my eyes. "I see you discovering your vandalized car, then filling out a police report. Later, I see you bitching about it over breakfast in my camper."

"You promised you would teach me to surf," she said.

"I saw that, also. Telling the future, one has to be selective, or it comes out babble. You have to tell just the edge, like in a Hemingway story."

"Smartass, if you can't zip it, wait outside," Madame Tammy said, offering me a Pabst and pointing. "Having nonbelievers around sours my psychic zone."

"I am what I am."

"Who ain't?" The fortune-teller waved her gnarled hand at the love seat. "Park it."

I had never seen a reading before. Madame Tammy put Janine's hands flat on the table. Then the old woman took up her Tarot deck and dealt out a dozen cards, face up. Janine leaned in close as the psychic brooded. Madame Tammy had somehow achieved clarity of mind, despite the hour, the alcohol, and the smoke. She sensed the cards' gravity and began to mumble.

"What is it?" Janine said. "Is it bad?"

"Just give me a second," Madame Tammy said. "There's a good reading in here somewhere."

Later, as we drove toward my place with an orange sun rising in the east, it wasn't clear whether Janine would stay. She drove too fast on the empty beach road, talking angrily, upset about the future predicted for her. It's just one more bad sign when the psychic refuses payment.

"Fucking Death? What the fuck is that all about?"

In this edition of cards he'd ridden a gaunt black horse, worn silver armor, had a skull for a head, and reached out a skeletal hand at a man lying in a pool of blood on the road. Madame Tammy had explained that the Death card wasn't necessarily bad, that the figure of Death often signaled an impending change.

"Everyone knows that Death isn't meant to be read literally," I said. "They did years ago, anyway. It's like a metaphor."

"I was in fifth grade ten years ago," she said. "And if it's not a bad card, why is the guy on the road covered in blood?"

"Maybe he's hurt, and Death's doing the right thing. He's offering him a lift."

Janine glared at me. "That doesn't help. I always get the bum deal. That's my fate. The cards were just a reminder of what I already know. I get upset about that."

"You shouldn't."

She narrowed her eyes and said, "I am what I am." She said it in a mocking tone, but the voice was enough hers that, for a fraction of a second, she became Elise, animated and talking. I can still see her that way, wearing clothes my fiancée would never have worn, driving a car the likes of which she'd never had, in a part of the country she hated, like a moment from a parallel world in which she still lived.

I grabbed Janine by the shoulder and kissed her mouth. She parted her lips to let me taste lip balm and sour beer, then grabbed the back of my head, kissing me and pulling my head down so she could see while she braked. The beach road was clear, and the sun was coming up on the condominiums on the beach and the neighborhoods of shabby houses. There was no one around to see us groping each other, locked in fantasies allowed by how little we knew of each other.

In the apartment of the man I'd come to think of as my fiancée's murderer, the police found a diary filled with observations about Elise. There were even photographs and transcriptions of conversations he'd had with her. It was evident from his notes that he had been a regular at the café where she waited tables in a white blouse and black pants, where she pinned her hair, looking almost like someone else. This other woman, this waitress, was the one the murderer loved, or so I told myself, believing he'd had no real intimacy with her, until a detective let me see his diary. Why the detective did this I do not know—he had a plain face with the look of just having dropped his smile—and I looked back on it as an act of cruelty, though of course my spite was mixed with gratitude. Maybe he thought it would jog my memory, make me reveal something crucial to the case. Or maybe he was attempting kindness, trying to say the murderer was my male inferior. But all the diary did was leave me with more questions. According to its pages, Elise knew her killer's name. She flirted with him and told him details of our private life. She talked about our fights and made allusions to the sex we had. In trying to determine the amount of fantasy in the descriptions, I only grew more doubtful. Why hadn't she mentioned him? How much had she kept from me?

Most disturbing were the photographs. Some were several years old and could only have come from her apartment. The detectives had a theory that he'd found a way to get in and steal so few things that no one would notice. But I wondered whether she'd given them to him for some unimaginable reason. There were pictures of her parents and her sister, even one of me eating cereal from a mixing bowl once when I had a hilariously bad hangover. They were all pictures I was familiar with, ones she and I had looked at with enough attention to make them part of us. It seemed she would have noticed they were gone.

I did remember something then. It struck me as crucial to understanding what had happened, though the detective was not interested. My fiancée had been a beautiful woman and, before that, a very pretty girl. She told me once that all her life there had been men who breathed on the other end of the telephone line, who drove by her house at night, who followed her in public places and went out of their ways to put themselves in the line of her vision. There had always been men who showed up, uninvited, to visit her in places, at work and parties, at her parents' house when she was young and the driveway was empty of cars. She spoke about these men and boys with something like nostalgia, as if she both pitied and enjoyed their obsessions and missed them now that they were gone.

"Don't get so jealous," she told me one time as we lay together on the couch. "They're nothing compared to you. You're not in competition with them or anyone."

"What's that supposed to mean?" I asked.

She gave me one of her cryptic little smiles. "You actually caught me."

Back at my camper, we didn't bother to go in. We were both more than primed, and I carried Janine through the dunes as she held her arms around my neck and kissed me. It was like something out of a romantic comedy, except we were going to fuck. It was high tide, and we found a spot between ghost crab burrows.

Afterward, Janine shook the sand out of her clothes and got dressed. She was tired and annoyed by how much sand had gotten into her hair and by the after-sex silence that had descended. She seemed nervous I would now reveal my true identity as a jerk.

"Let's go for a swim," I said. "We'll have your first surfing lesson."

She raised her eyebrows and gave me a slight frown. "I need to sleep right now. I get really cranky when I don't get enough sleep."

This was very different from Elise, who had always been willing to stay up for another round, who had been my partner in putting many parties to bed. Janine scratched in her hair, knocking loose little deposits of sand, and scowled to show her disgust. She was at a loss for how to go to bed and was pouting severely until she saw my hammock hanging between two palms. She looked back, smiling tentatively. "Can I sleep in that without being eaten alive?"

Since I had to work in two hours, I decided against sleep and took my surfboard down to the water. The water was moving out, giving rise to short stubborn waves that were just enough to stand up on and ride for a few seconds. It required enough effort to take my mind off the strangeness of the future, and altogether it was a good morning. The murky green water radiated out beneath me in uneven planes of waves and wavelets, a heap of broken glass outlined by the sun. I pretended Janine was Elise asleep and felt a burst of strength. Crashing waves and crying seagulls evoked the steady indolence of an early Friday night, when everything is calm, in anticipation of going out to the unknown. I skated around on my board, looking shoreward. Janine hung between the palms like a hooked sardine.

Though I've always assumed each person is unique, Elise believed in types. We used to argue about it. I took the position that she couldn't put people into neat categories, while she argued that I was putting off critical thinking in the interest of naïve openness, which was no different, she said, than a kind of enthusiastic idiocy. This was the flip side of the kindness that dominated her personality—a disappointed honesty that would tear out your heart as if it were a Post-it note. I would get angry and tell her to describe some of these types, and she would always start with heroes and villains.

"Heroes and villains?" I said once, when I was tired of hearing her recount the same old list. "That sounds like a fucking *Jeopardy* category. What the fuck do those terms even mean?"

"The really good guys," she said lightly, "and the really, really bad ones."

"Something tells me there's a reference to me here," I said.

She shrugged.

"Come on. I'm one of the good guys, right?"

She just winked and gave me a kiss on the throat.

Janine moved her two small suitcases into my camper with the intention of staying the week. She was going to be in Cocoa Beach, anyway, she said. When I asked why she was in town she shrugged and opened the refrigerator to see what there was to drink. She seemed like she was used to having things her way.

The longer she stayed, the less she reminded me of Elise. It was obvious from her car and her clothes and her manners that she came from money. She had expensive tastes that she indulged with her own money at meat and fish markets, and she insisted that we cook supper at night. When I teased her for priding herself on being able to follow recipes, she smiled condescendingly, for to her I was a surfer who worked as a lifeguard, a simple beast of the seashore, a dependent of burrito shops. She had no way of knowing how carefully I'd invested or about the financial work I did out west, and I had no intention of telling her. Both of us were happy with our secrets, and we avoided talking about the past, which could only get in the way of the surfing and screwing. During my watch she would lie out, the only sunbather on the beach, and when Chuck stopped his truck by my chair to talk, I sensed his eyes looking at her from behind his mirrored sunglasses. Otherwise Janine and I were alone.

After the fourth day I began to feel the inevitability of the end. Though she never answered her phone when it rang, Janine would immediately play her messages, her face setting grimly as she listened. Something was wrong, but I never pushed her to tell me about it. Not only was I afraid that asking would encourage her to leave, but I'd been through enough therapy to know sharing was overrated for people who already knew how to communicate.

On our eighth day together, I'd closed the perpetually unvisited beach and was putting five ears of corn onto the grill when Janine said we had to talk.

It was inevitable, but I didn't have to like it. "So talk."

"No, I mean it. We need to discuss some things."

"You've been in the camper," I said. "I don't exactly have a den."

"Right here is fine." She drew a line in the sand with her big toe and looked up at me. The sun was going down and violet light surrounded us, bluing the palm trunks. "I don't want to go into it, but my family's all fucked up," she said. "They've sent someone down here to get me."

"To 'get' you?"

She was serious. "He's a private investigator. He's kind of dangerous. Not to me."

"So what?" Reluctant to hear this, I shook salt out over the corn, even though it just fell on the husks. "How's he going to find you out here?"

"Dennis, come on. People have seen us in public. The city is tiny. There are like five real bars."

"It doesn't matter. You're an adult."

"You ever hear of adult kidnapping?"

"That's bull," I said. "You're my witness to that."

"But they can make it difficult for you. And Willis could hurt you. Really hurt you."

"Willis? His name is Willis?"

"And there's the car. It's mine, but it's in my dad's name."

"So?"

"So they can say it's stolen."

"So abandon it."

"Dennis, this is serious."

"So what?" I said. I stared at the fire lapping up around the whitening coals. I knew she was saying she had to leave. "So what? What do I care? How do you want your hamburger cooked?"

She touched my arm, and I finally looked at her. What I saw surprised me. Here was a young woman looking at me with a scolding impatience, resembling no one I'd known.

The next morning she got up before sunrise to pack her car. She laughed at my ridiculous offer of blankets and food, which was more for my own comfort than for hers. She had gone into a new state of mind, a high-energy departure mode, and was reluctant to acknowledge me, as if I'd only slow her down. She brushed past me with her suitcases and ignored me when I said her name, then ran back into the camper for a last check. She wanted to be gone already, I realized, and so I simply waited by her car.

She came out of the camper, play-pouting, making big sad eyes at me. I just stared at her.

She sighed. "Listen. If Willis comes around here looking for you, give me a call to let me know you're okay. And if he doesn't come around, give me a call anyhow." She took my phone from my pocket and entered her information into it.

"Don't you want mine?"

She waved her hand dismissively. "I'll get it when you call."

"If I call."

She raised her eyebrows as if there were no other possibility. "Oh. You'll call."

"Tell me something," I said. "Your parents have sent this Willis guy after you before. How often do you do this?"

She broke into a full smile. She had made herself up for the road and was looking quite beautiful in a soft brown trapeze dress. "I am what I am," she said, wrinkling her nose as she pulled free of my hands.

After she'd gone I had to go down to the beach to work. As usual, it was empty, and I put out the orange flags and rescue buoys and radioed in that the beach was officially open. It was a cool, windy morning, and dark clouds were moving swiftly out to sea, so fast that the cape was unlikely to get any of the rain they carried. I was standing out on the chair, watching distant black dolphins leap out of the troubled water, when Chuck drove up to the stand. I pulled down the hood of my sweatshirt and climbed down to talk to him at his rolled-down window.

He looked worried. "Where's the girl?"

"Gone. About an hour ago."

"I hope so, man. We have a missing persons APB this morning for a Janine Devereaux. I don't know if she told you that was her name, but it's the girl who's been staying with you. Down to the last detail." He showed me the printout of a sorority photo in which Janine had parted her hair down the middle and wore an ivory blouse and a strand of pearls. As a sorority girl, Elise would have had a distinct sex appeal.

"She's definitely on the freeway by now."

Chuck took the picture away, and I guessed his eyes were angry behind those big sunglasses. "Is she really gone, Dennis?" he said, trying to sound tough. "I'd hate to have to arrest you."

"Cut it out. She left less than an hour ago," I told him. "I tried to stop her."

He hissed out a breath. "You should count your blessings. I don't know who these people are, but all the police chiefs are on the phone this morning. There's something big going on."

"Not really," I said. "Nothing that hasn't happened before."

Around eleven that night I was sitting in the dark camper, watching a fuzzy detective show on the television, when a car passed on the road with no headlights, which in the Florida woods at night could only be intentional. I quickly went to the camper door and let myself out. The door was lightweight and easy to close without a sound. I made it to the palms where my hammock was tied and waited until I heard the soft footsteps coming through the Bermuda grass.

An immense man went to my camper door and began rapping impatiently on the hollow metal. He called out, "Hello, hello? Anybody home?" A moment later he drew what I assumed was a gun from the region of his waist, tried the knob, and opened the door wide. For a moment he stood at the step below the door, looking into the camper, and I got a look at half of his grinning face, one eye bright with lizard mischief shining darkly out of thick folds of gray skin. Gun out before him, he went inside and shut the door and locked it.

I stood back behind the trees, knowing that when he came out he'd be blind in the night. My body had gone numb with fright and something else which made it tolerable. The camper shook as this guy Willis went back and forth inside, and then the lights inside went out, and the trailer was still for what must have been a few minutes.

He must have waited until his eyes adjusted to the darkness, because he emerged suddenly and stepped out into the yard, a shifting inky giant with wide elbows holding a gun out in front of him. He didn't bother closing the trailer door, and he lingered in front of it, as if he thought I might try to slip past him and back inside. In the dark he was a hulk, a bogeyman whose heavy breathing rose above the sound of the insects. After a while he seemed to accept that I was not going to confront him, and he began to taunt me. "Come on, Denny," he said. "Don't you want to save Janine from the big bad wolf? Maybe she'll let you stick it in her one more time if you play the big huntsman." He let out a deep-throated giggle. "Probably not, though. She's probably forgotten all about you already. But that's not what this is really about, is it?"

I must have reacted with an exhale or a small movement, because he sensed the direction in which I was hiding, and turned to address me. His smile was audible in his voice. "It is remarkable, how much she resembles Elise, isn't it? It really is something how much two people can look alike. But you know what, Denny? It's not that strange, really it's not. When you get into my line of work, you see that it's actually pretty goddamn commonplace." He paused, listening, then resumed. "Although what you did is pretty strange, a little perverse. I'll have to tell Janine all about it when I see her."

He put one foot back then, bracing himself, as if expecting me to burst out of the darkness to fight for her honor, or for Elise's or for my own. When I did not appear, he gave a sigh. Gradually, the dark ridge of his shoulders relaxed, and he lowered his gun. His voice no longer smiled when he said, "Well, Denny. You are strange."

I stood in the dark yard long after he had trudged off through the grass and driven away to where I no longer heard his car. At first I remained still out of caution, afraid it was an illusion he had contrived and that he was still there, just beyond the far side of the camper, waiting for me to move. Slowly I began to accept that I was alone. A long time passed, and then something did move across the open yard. It was a possum with three babies in tow, clumsily ambling over the earth. They were nearly to the grill when I stepped out from the trees and scared them into a run. For the animals, it was just another night in the woods.

My camper felt unsafe for the night, so I headed down to the beach. Waves smacked ashore, and the lifeguard chair stood facing the horizon, where ocean and sky muddled in darkness. I thought I might sleep up there, where I'd be hidden from sight by the backrest. But once I climbed up and felt the wind on my face, I began to think about going into town instead. It was still early, after all, and in the bars the night was only beginning. Still I felt no rush to call a taxi. I felt rich in time. It would be a while before women got up from their chairs to dance where there was no dance floor. I wondered if Willis had been telling the truth, if all the cities and towns were full of people just like Elise and me, if what we all thought was secret was a myth we told each other behind closed doors. Maybe all that stood between the finance guy I'd been and the lifeguard I'd become was this surfer boy disguise and the impulse to try it on.

I took out my phone and called Janine as promised. The signal on the beach was weak, and when I got her voicemail, waves of static interfered with the recorded greeting. "Hey, it's me," said a distant female voice. It could have been anyone. "After the beep, you can tell me all about it."

Messages from the beach always came through unclear, and I doubted she would know my voice. At any rate I had nothing more to say to her. I left a message for Elise, telling her how much I missed her, and then I put my phone away.

THE FLANNERY O'CONNOR AWARD
FOR SHORT FICTION

David Walton, *Evening Out*

Leigh Allison Wilson, *From the Bottom Up*

Sandra Thompson, *Close-Ups*

Susan Neville, *The Invention of Flight*

Mary Hood, *How Far She Went*

François Camoin, *Why Men Are Afraid of Women*

Molly Giles, *Rough Translations*

Daniel Curley, *Living with Snakes*

Peter Meinke, *The Piano Tuner*

Tony Ardizzone, *The Evening News*

Salvatore La Puma, *The Boys of Bensonhurst*

Melissa Pritchard, *Spirit Seizures*

Philip F. Deaver, *Silent Retreats*

Gail Galloway Adams, *The Purchase of Order*

Carole L. Glickfeld, *Useful Gifts*

Antonya Nelson, *The Expendables*

Nancy Zafris, *The People I Know*

Debra Monroe, *The Source of Trouble*

Robert H. Abel, *Ghost Traps*

T. M. McNally, *Low Flying Aircraft*

Alfred DePew, *The Melancholy of Departure*

Dennis Hathaway, *The Consequences of Desire*

Rita Ciresi, *Mother Rocket*

Dianne Nelson, *A Brief History of Male Nudes in America*

Christopher McIlroy, *All My Relations*

Alyce Miller, *The Nature of Longing*

Carol Lee Lorenzo, *Nervous Dancer*

C. M. Mayo, *Sky over El Nido*

Wendy Brenner, *Large Animals in Everyday Life*

Paul Rawlins, *No Lie Like Love*

Harvey Grossinger, *The Quarry*

Ha Jin, *Under the Red Flag*

Andy Plattner, *Winter Money*

Frank Soos, *Unified Field Theory*

Mary Clyde, *Survival Rates*

Hester Kaplan, *The Edge of Marriage*

Darrell Spencer, *CAUTION Men in Trees*

Robert Anderson, *Ice Age*

Bill Roorbach, *Big Bend*

Dana Johnson, *Break Any Woman Down*

Gina Ochsner, *The Necessary Grace to Fall*

Kellie Wells, *Compression Scars*

Eric Shade, *Eyesores*

Catherine Brady, *Curled in the Bed of Love*

Ed Allen, *Ate It Anyway*

Gary Fincke, *Sorry I Worried You*

Barbara Sutton, *The Send-Away Girl*

David Crouse, *Copy Cats*

Randy F. Nelson, *The Imaginary Lives of Mechanical Men*

Greg Downs, *Spit Baths*

Peter LaSalle, *Tell Borges If You See Him:
Tales of Contemporary Somnambulism*

Anne Panning, *Super America*

Margot Singer, *The Pale of Settlement*

Andrew Porter, *The Theory of Light and Matter*

Peter Selgin, *Drowning Lessons*

Geoffrey Becker, *Black Elvis*

Lori Ostlund, *The Bigness of the World*

Linda LeGarde Grover, *The Dance Boots*

Jessica Treadway, *Please Come Back to Me*

Amina Gautier, *At-Risk*

Melinda Moustakis, *Bear Down, Bear North*

E. J. Levy, *Love, in Theory*

Hugh Sheehy, *The Invisibles*